THE RIFT

EⅬ

EMERGENT LITERATURES

Emergent Literatures is a series of international scope that makes available, in English, works of fiction that have been ignored or excluded because of their difference from established models of literature.

The Rift
V. Y. Mudimbe

Gates of the City
Elias Khoury

Yes, Comrade!
Manuel Rui

The Alexander Plays
Adrienne Kennedy

Deadly Triplets
Adrienne Kennedy

Human Mourning
José Revueltas

Love in Two Languages
Abdelkebir Khatibi

The Stream of Life
Clarice Lispector

Little Mountain
Elias Khoury

The Passion according to G. H.
Clarice Lispector

An American Story
Jacques Godbout

The Trickster of Liberty
Gerald Vizenor

In One Act
Adrienne Kennedy

The Rift

V. Y. Mudimbe

Translated by
Marjolijn de Jager

University of Minnesota Press

Minneapolis

London

Originally published as *L'Ecart* by Editions Présence Africaine. Paris, 1979.

Published by the University of Minnesota Press
2037 University Avenue Southeast, Minneapolis, MN 55455-3092
Printed in the United States of America on acid-free paper

Library of Congress Cataloging-in-Publication Data

Mudimbe, V. Y., 1941-
   [Ecart. English]
   The rift / V. Y. Mudimbe; translated by Marjolijn de Jager.
      p.   cm.—(Emergent literatures)
   Translation of: L'écart.
   ISBN 0-8166-2312-0
   I. Title. II. Series.
PQ3989.2.M77E2513   1993
843–dc20   92-44511
                                                    CIP

I

September 7, 197 . . .

Exhaustion . . . My exhaustion . . . weighs me down so much . . . Like yesterday, the day before, a month ago . . . A heavy weight in the atmosphere tense with the heat. The air-conditioning is working irregularly and with its noisy fits and starts is stirring up my helplessness and my rage: since the very beginning of the hot season they have promised to repair it . . . What a farce . . . And I keep waiting, exasperated by their unnecessary lies: "It's a promise, my dear Nara, we'll bring it back to life . . . get it working again . . . You'll see, tomorrow, the day after at the latest . . . " No matter how much I beg for a change of rooms . . . "But, my dear Nara, tomorrow your air-conditioning will be in full working order; come now, a little patience . . . " And I give in, like a good boy: humiliated by my own inability to scream at them that I've had enough of these promises, ashamed of my complacency and resignation, of which this thug of a landlord takes full advantage. I ought to have the courage to raise my voice and tell him what I think of this rat hole that he so pompously calls a hotel . . .

"So, Nara? Still at the hotel?"—"Well, yeah, still in my hole . . . " Some half-unpacked boxes . . . An unfinished flight of stairs . . . Walls suffering from eczema . . . The stone floor, once beige, now discolored . . . and more cracks than anything else. You have to live in it to believe it. Every time I go up to this room I am surprised that I am not more shocked than I am. The ceiling is an oozing wound that seeps water when it rains . . . Only my intemperance saves me . . . A small table, a chair, a hard bed . . . And piles of books everywhere . . . They are both a bewilderment and my shelter . . . All that is just fine. I would accept this false paradise if only the air-conditioning were working . . . Torture? . . . No. Not even that. A disappointment brought to new life every time the landlord lies to me again. And instead of yelling at him, I give in every time and feel guilty. As if I were the one to blame. It is true . . . I am not innocent . . . Like all adults. But is that a reason? Of course, there is the shibboleth from the *Manual of Decomposition*[1] that calls for me to be patient . . . "One is civilized only to the extent that one does not loudly voice one's leprosy . . . " Why should they impose pustules on me besides? With the weather we're having, the malfunctioning of an air conditioner is really quite a scene . . . "Are you working, Nara?"—"What do you think?"—"We don't see you anymore . . . " That's for sure. You have to love your own wreckage . . . And then the gray wrath of the ants . . . The tropical fog that rises with the early night . . . A gift . . .

While I wait, I should really calm down. Be able to take stock of the day. Retain what is essential. And, to this end, begin at the beginning, reconstruct the day minute by minute, from the moment of getting up, name all my actions, remember my thoughts, express my feelings and reactions to people and things, then eliminate what is unnecessary, and enter what is important. If I remember correctly, that is the method for responsible conduct in life that I learned at school.

There was the always recurring misery of every one of my awakenings and then . . . And then I dragged around like a robot, as usual. There was the early morning humidity, the overcrowded bus. That strong smell of packed hu-

1. Emile Cioran, *Précis de decomposition*, 1949.—TRANS.

manity . . . Finally, there were the hours spent in the library that come back to me in a great wave of revulsion.

As I arrived there, I thought I would pick up the rhythm of my work as it was before: fill out incomplete index cards, put together a program, overcome the crisis at last that has paralyzed me for nine months . . . Yes, see myself make some progress with this dissertation that I've been trailing behind me for almost ten years now . . . The archivist welcomed me with kindness. He seemed intrigued by my disappearing act . . . "You're coming back to us?" — "Yes," I said, "I've been traveling."

He shook my hand emphatically as if he wanted to tell me a secret . . . or something else . . . I tried to catch his eye, unsuccessfully. He avoided my look. I only caught a glimpse of his teeth, badly yellowed from smoking. I hardly recognized them. They used to seem beautifully white to me before. I was probably wrong. He seemed to have lost a good deal of weight: his face had lost its fullness . . . He is turning into a mummy . . . And again I felt the pressure of his hand, more strongly still. "Well, don't break it for me," I said in embarrassment. — "Oh, no! Why not? I'm so happy to see you again. It's a year since you left us, isn't it?" — "Nine months, Salim, not a year . . . Long enough to carry a child to full term . . . "

He smiled again, generously showing me the dull purple of his gums. His still-furtive look seemed to take inventory of the space I occupied. In a voice of disbelief he repeated: "Nine months, that's all! Nine months . . . It isn't possible. Nine months, impossible . . . "

He shook his head. Then suddenly he left me alone to take his place again at the small desk that was his in a far corner between two sets of shelves. He began to arrange his cards. Just as before: his head, now slightly more balding, lightly bent to the left; with trembling hands and mumbling lips he seemed to be in conversation with the bits of pink cardboard he was handling. Still amazed by this peculiar welcome, I passed in front of Aminata's desk. I wanted to stop, pick up where we left off, say hello to her, but as I hesitated one second too long I found myself at an empty table next to the glass door that looks out over the small inner courtyard.

I took my index cards from my briefcase. I looked at the handwriting; it's small and I hate it. "You write badly . . . " — "I am modest, sir . . . " — "Excuse me?" — "I do try . . . " — "One wouldn't have thought so, Nara . . . " A pang . . . Of no importance . . . Penmanship is not punishment. Not yet . . . In order to inherit heaven . . . there was this decisive passageway: the art of the downstroke. Gesture corresponds to intention. What to do? Where to pick up the dialogue again with these notes that open a whole universe of contradictions for me? I was dreaming, yes, that's it . . . Interminable hallways, completely white, leading to realms unknown . . . It was important for me to find a rhythm again, to prescribe a specific movement for myself: reread, correct, see what merited revision and completion. Then, establish a daily work schedule and specific criteria for the interpretation of the data. No, beginning again seemed like a diversion to me. The overhead fan was turning, creaking lightly. Its circular motion became encrusted in me, gently, like tiny bites. And I began to watch the few people bent over their books: insects, indifferent to this noisy environment. A young woman was reading a paperback. She might have been a student on vacation. Two boys, side by side, engrossed in their reading of a kind of encyclopedic dictionary. What earthly use could they make of it? And, silently eloquent at his own small table, Salim, tormenting his pieces of cardboard.

Again the hallways asserted themselves. The humming noise of cars came in from the outside. The throttling of a truck, on its last legs. I wanted to decode this life that was making me suffer and, in the courtyard, I came upon a broom, a bucket, an old abandoned crate. On a board you could still read BIBLIOTHEQUE NAT . . . I knew very well that I should finish this word off, refused to, though I'd already done so at the beginning. Finish off would surely mean an address or a body. But to what end? Was it not more my style to let things be? I wanted to lose myself in a small pile of sweepings, forgotten beside the bucket. A dirty pink . . . Tiny black spots here and there . . . Like bits of soot . . . Trails . . . As on the bucket: light bumps and mud spots giving it the look of flesh tortured by time. I wanted to follow the lines in the pavement and instead found the hallways again. Piles of dirty sheets stacked along a wall. A painting: the face of a one-eyed woman with a contemptuous mouth. A hardboard suitcase in front of a door . . . Light bulbs glaring. I tighten my fists . . . Come on now . . . There is no reason . . . Voices . . . Very close . . . "My son had an excellent education in Germany." — "So he is an engineer?" — "No, a historian." — "Oh, really! I thought, though . . . " A book falls . . . a dull noise . . . A marvelous smack . . . I had made a clumsy movement . . . The hallways are filled . . . Bewildered couples . . . A man with a coarse face . . . Hard . . . He is holding a woman by the shoulders . . . She is in tears . . . He lets go of her . . . One step backwards . . . He pounces on her . . . I close my eyes . . .

It was the alarm. I shook my head several times. Accidentally I caught Aminata's glance; she was observing me. I gave her a bored smile. By following the hallways, I might as easily end up in a vipers' nest as in a chicken coop. How does one choose between a lethal bite and infernal twitter-

11

ing? To these morbid assertions I would have preferred the evocation of no matter what other illusion: a woman's name, the warm sand of a beach somewhere, or the delirium of a drunken evening.

Aminata, the eyes of the others. I see her and sense that she is assuming control of me again. In spite of myself. She takes advantage of a power that I would have liked to rip away from her. In the name of harmony. She exploits everything: disasters as well as happiness, absentmindedness and gossip . . . I can hear her already with her firm and loud voice: "Nara this, Nara that . . . " And tomorrow my few friends will be looking for news, their eyes concerned, their ears flapping. Just because I was shaking my head in the library . . . "It was the rhythm of a quartet, believe me . . . Dvořák's quartet for piano . . . I heard it recently . . . It keeps haunting me . . . I can see myself still hearing it inside my head, sixty years from now, after listening to it this time . . . Music . . . It is a kingdom, without doubt the only one that is truly fascinating. Its pillars, its rustic lanes give voice to a spell . . . "—"Dvořák?"—"Yes . . . the temperature of a farewell . . . of every sincere goodbye . . . "

Soon it will be ten in the evening . . . I am caught in these memories, am going in circles. As I was leaving my hotel this morning, I thought I could catch up on the time I've lost . . . Work on putting my card file in order. Can't be helped. I just don't feel right. It's all very good and well to tell myself that sleep might be a proper refuge, but there, too, is a barrier. I mean: laziness. The utter boredom of the daily ritual: get up, open the kitchen cabinet (?) to find a bottle of phenobarbital, take a pill with water from the faucet, tepid water . . . No thanks. As late as possible . . . Flee from this steam room? All I'd need is a bit of courage to join Soum and Camara at the Soleil Rouge for some fun and beer. Slight inebriation would reconcile me with the world. But the mere thought of having to put on my shoes to go out weighs me down. And then, too, since I have no money, as usual, I would have to feel truly inspired to make Soum treat me, promising him very sincerely, as always, that the next round is mine. The round that will never come. What to do?

At least, noting down these few dead-end alleys where my helplessness leads me gives me something to do, and it consoles me that I am still able to name some of my longings. Like the one that has kept me riveted, for some years now, to those tropical ethnic groups that are fenced in by the Rivers Sankuru to the north, the Kasai to the west, the Lukibu to the east, the Lulua to the south, and the Dibese Forest to the southeast. They have been studied before, I know that. I have gone through the work of the ethnologists on several occasions, gone back to all of their sources with great care, have even forced the secret doors of esoteric articles written in Dutch. I would like to start from scratch, reconstruct the universe of these peoples from start to finish: decolonize the knowledge already gathered about them, bring to light new, more believable genealogies, and be able to advance an interpretation that pays more careful attention to their environment and their true history. Often I find myself to be surprisingly hesitant. At such moments I feel like making fun of this unyielding ambition to make new inroads. But terrorized by I know not what, I tell myself that, as I come out of a fit of laughter, I would perhaps risk finding myself face to face with grimacing masks of Kuba slaves, buried alive at Nyimi's death.[2]

2. King of the Kuba, God on earth, he is the image and the symbol of divine omnipotence. His full title is Nyimi Bushong Ntshieme Nkontsh.

The service of the king is, in fact, eternal. I should describe and not profane it.

Fear their competitiveness . . . Their insolence as well. It is nauseating . . . "What's the point? The Kuba are well known . . . They've been studied in depth . . . " — "By a black?" — "Do you think that would change anything . . . ?" — "First let the Germans be happy with the descriptions of their past by the French . . . and the French with English studies about them . . . Only then will I concede . . . I do believe, sir, that sensitivity is terribly important." — "That's a viewpoint to maintain . . . and to foster . . . Sensitivity is a freedom that is both precious and irreplaceable . . . One needs the irreverence of sacrilege to imagine that . . . Obviously, Africa seen from the outside is nothing but a map . . . Rivers . . . Mountains . . . Tribes . . . Without the brutish past the West assigns to it . . . All right . . . "

It was Aminata, boiling with rage, who read me the riot act last year: "Watch out for the dead, they sometimes turn back." No other image would have been more powerful. She forced me to become heedful again and I stopped entertaining Salim with the barbarism of the funeral rites of Nyimi. Once again I found the path of silence and sympathy. The contact with a tradition and the practice of its rigors had to subject me to its norms so that my words could represent them faithfully.

It is now eleven o'clock.

Go out? The Soleil Rouge is just becoming lively. As Soum says, this is the finest hour, eleven at night. Lovely bodies available everywhere. Exotic dances on the terrace in honor of the tourists. Inside the place, the obligatory rainbow lights conjure up the night. The beer flows freely and explodes the inhibitions. And then there is the indescribable throng of bodies sweating life. I can see Soum and Camara creating the occasion . . . As usual: surrounded by beautiful women, laughing broadly, their arms out wide, their looks innocent and obscene at the same time, like those of young communicants.

Should I go? I would really like to. But then I must decide to leave this little table where I'm writing. And face the night. It's always the same: diving into the darkness seems an act of insanity to me. No, I'm lying. The darkness is a trap, rather, and I'm afraid of it . . . It is about two miles before I'll reach the first lighted street. Once there, I'll easily catch a bus and be in the center of town in less than an hour. A few minutes walking . . . then there is the Soleil Rouge and, at one of the tables, Soum and Camara's warm friendship to welcome me.

But before that happiness, hell comes first, the real test, as Dr. Sano keeps repeating . . . "Come now, Nara, you should have overcome that obstacle already . . . " Overcome! That's just lovely. Also, easy for him to say. He cannot understand that one might consider the night, any night, a mortal enemy. How do you overcome that?

"Are you familiar with the night, Dr. Sano? No, you're not, are you? I, on the other hand, know it all too well: we've met. And very early on. I was six years old, Dr. Sano . . . A Saturday morning. It's seven o'clock or seven-thirty . . . While making breakfast, my mother notices that the jam jar is empty. She doesn't yell. She calls me: "Nara, you again." I deny it. No use. Yet, the guilty one is my older brother: the night before, he had his friends over . . . I saw it all . . . I dare not tell on him. He'd beat me up . . . Do you understand? She punishes me: locks me up in the tool closet . . . Forgets me there for several days . . . Well, that's what I thought: several days, a night without end . . . And there was a rat in there, yes, a rat . . . When she came to set me free she was in tears. She begged me to forgive her for having forgotten me for an entire day. She said she had planned to let me out by noon at the latest. But something terrible had happened: I had hardly been locked up when they came to tell her that my father had died . . . He was on night duty on the construction site of the Maritime Company. She supposedly lost her head . . . In any case, I didn't see my dead father: what I saw in his bed was a huge rat; that is what I saw before I took to my heels . . . Do you understand, Dr. Sano?"

And now this as well: besides the heat, which is killing me, we now have mosquitoes, too. If I turn off the light and go to sleep, it would be pure torture. But do I have a choice? Perhaps between restaurant and theater . . . Baudelaire or Senghor? The glamour of school . . . A bulldozer . . . The mystery of choice seems rather shallow . . . After all, school doesn't have much meaning yet in the tropics . . . The main point is to live . . . or to survive . . . What choice is there? The methods for clearing a path through the forest constitute both a science and an art . . . The same is true for the way in which we cope with shame or make ourselves speak slowly . . . What we need in order to comment on the colors of appearances is the lavish grandiloquence of today's philosophers . . . The boundaries have certainly grown blurry . . . Does that prove that heaven is less high? The darkness stretches farther . . . Am I, then, going to set a price on it? A Dionysian arc rises up against rationality; the congeniality of folk music against the law . . . And even exaggeration becomes a gash that opens the door to the intoxication of harmonic tones . . . And I'm supposed to choose!

Just a few years ago, wasn't I forced to stud my dreams with stars within a closed range?

At school, the teachers clipped my wings: I had to devote myself to memorizing sentences, every day of an interminable childhood. My writing slate on my knees, the loneliness of the savanna in my heart, year after year I drew the successive waves of words. The wise men didn't even make me confident: first of all there was language, French . . . A disarray into which I had to inscribe my anguish . . . The sun everywhere, the putrid alleys of my neighborhood, the distorted mirrors of the stories told around the fire in the evenings became forbidden roads from one year to the next. My fevers, like my terrors, diminished with time. I banished them to the deepest corner of my consciousness. I was to become the son of a newly acquired knowledge.

And then there was the lengthy stay among the Toubab.[3] Five winters, cold and gray. One passion kept me going: to penetrate the mysteries of the places of science, so that one day I would turn this seemingly firm ground over. But this willpower showed cracks. During long, solitary nights I foresaw other dawns . . . I almost reconciled myself to my past. It was shaped like an enormous cemetery. I was a prisoner, standing in an endless line. The sky hung low. Some dried-up trees, blackened by the air, contrasted sharply with the layer of snow. They looked like the arms of praying figures asking for an impossible blessing. A despair that took on the colors of my distress. My own turn came: I moved forward to the grave . . . It was already half-filled with earth and snow . . . All in black, her body rigid, her eyes hard and dry, my mother looked at me: "Come on, quickly, throw your bit of soil and disappear . . . "

Should I listen to her? Right away I understood that I was going to disappear underneath a mound of earth. That only a scandal would save me perhaps. And I howled.

3. In certain parts of Africa, during the period of colonialism, white people were referred to as Toubab.

Once I stopped shrieking, I found myself behind bars, like a wild beast . . . "Isabelle, do you see the choice I am left with?"—"I'll put on a record, Nara. I'm sure you'll like it . . . "

I was watching her: she was engrossed in the movements of the cantata, which was growing louder. Her full lips slightly apart showed a glimpse of her teeth, shiny, strong, firmly implanted. "Isabelle, you have the mouth of a Negress . . . "

My haven exploded because of this unfortunate compliment. She got up, her ears red, her eyes ablaze. It made no sense combined with this cantata purifying the night. I became panic-stricken: had I kept silent, would I not have been better off? She came toward me with trembling hands. My throat dry, I watched the anger in her eyes grow. Behind her, the pale green curtains were moving in the wind. I was intrigued: what could she do to me? My compliment seemed to have insulted her. Fine. So that was it, an offended princess . . . Was that all? A passage from my school days came back to me . . . By a certain Archambault: "This Cythera they call enchanted, look at it . . . It is, after all, nothing more than a bit of soil. How can we adore Venus when she has come to us in the form of a tale-telling Negress, thievish and dumb, who has captivated us by the shape of her haunches, the scent of her hair, and the texture of her skin?"

She was either going to hit me or tell me to leave. How should I react and still keep my dignity? Her long hair, the color of burned flesh (?), bounced on her naked shoulders. For the first time, I was struck by the regularity of her body: the long, full legs beautifully complemented an ample chest. I got up, ready for a confrontation, resolved neither to ask her pardon nor to refer to the confessions of the past few days. Is there a formula for every occasion? . . .

Did I ever know a single one that could protect me against all disasters? The storm is rumbling . . . the thunder will soon break loose . . . And the only thing that worries me is how I will figure out what it is I must do! . . . "You know?"—"I don't . . . Tell me . . . "—"Oh yes, you do . . . What a ham you are!"—"And you aren't? I'm going to kiss you, and I'll know, won't I?"—"Yes . . . "

The wait is coming to an end, a net is being woven . . . The mesh tightens, becomes rigid . . . I let myself live in a state of surprise, and every time I promise myself to take the time needed to question the destiny that binds me to a woman . . . What understanding did we have that could still hold us together?

While I began to feel a bomb ready to explode inside my head, the improbable took place in front of me . . . She knelt down and clasped my legs. I crouched beside her and took her face in my hands: "What is the matter, Isabelle?" I asked myself: wasn't it from the depths of her hatred of Negroes that a strange desire had surged? "Make love to me, Nara . . . "

Pitiful, this choice . . . Mine . . . In ecstasy, her eyelids fluttered . . . My nerves were taut: I could feel the rocking of my head increase. Isabelle's eyes were nothing but a hollow filled with tears; her mouth a wide-open bay . . . I had to slide into it. Meet up with her on a shore that she had picked and know that I was, without any doubt, going to thwart her in a bestial taunting . . . I was a phallus . . . Could be nothing else . . . And the moans that I would be hearing, those cries that I would prefer never to have heard, would come forth from the joining of two realms, man and beast . . . And I had the choice . . .

As then, and as always, I would have to throw myself on an already established path. Populated with mosquitoes this time: that too is part of my calvary. My paradise begins where my hesitations end. There, worries become bells. They are ringing. To say that life flows, a spasmodic rough draft upon which I outline my name . . . The incompleteness of my dread accounts for a past: it is, surely, another form of self-reproach, but at least being able to interpret it would protect me, I hope, against the illusions of my spirit. I would have had neither the freedom to choose this hell nor the grace to be able to track the road to a possible paradise . . . "It's because I am black, Isabelle. Do you know what it is to be black?" — "Are you a masochist, Nara?" — "I think not . . . But you're right in bringing it up: masochist. That is to say, I think I'm scratching at a wound . . . But does that wound exist?" — "You're looking for allegations of racism."

She seemed sincere enough. In her company, my loneliness weighed more heavily. I watched her eat. I thought back to the road that had led me here: how could I forget? The outlines of a cruel absence, relentless excess, arrival of an oppression . . . That is what growing up means . . . From my village to the city, from the mosque to Catholic school . . . one single momentum . . . I had but one obsession . . . That pale light in the distance, at the end of that endless roadway, lined with eucalyptus . . . The call of the open fields . . . A distraction . . . evanescent, fleeting . . . The central path was to remain the goal . . . Remember: the stones in the roads, the thorns in the woods and my bleeding feet, and so forth. So, as the years went by, I had slid into another universe . . . That's where I was now, well shod, comfortably warm, learning how to eat Galway oysters . . . I gently pushed the flowerpot to the left in order to watch her more closely, that slightly fuzzy skin, that sweet little nose in a pink face, the hazel eyes that took on the hue of dried herbs in the electric light . . . "It's not a question of allegations, Isabelle. No, that's not it. I am the reason for the racism of others; I feel it because I exist and I am here . . . " — "You do exaggerate, Nara. Aren't you eating anymore? Don't you see that I . . . " — "We're not talking about you . . . but about me . . . Did you notice? When we went into that restaurant . . . Those eyes devouring us . . . You noticed, didn't you? What were they saying, those eyes? Did you even get it?" — "We make an extraordinary couple, that's all. A rare couple . . . We arouse the curiosity of other people . . . "

She was being stupid. I have a toothache . . . "You should take some cortisol . . . One tablet every two hours . . . " I have a sore throat . . . "Some cortisol, every two hours . . . Suck on it . . . Let it dissolve slowly in your mouth. You do know what I'm saying? You mustn't swallow it . . . " I have an earache . . . "Did you take some cortisol?" Stupid . . . "That's all I ever take . . . " — "Ah, then all is well . . . " — "Are you prescribing it?" — "It is a synthetic steroid, an intensely active antiflogiston with minimal electrolytic disequilibrium . . . " — "Ah, very well. It's effective then, Doctor?" Stupid . . . That restaurant . . . It seems that the season is mild . . . Strollers with dogs on the leash fill the sidewalks . . . Naked backs . . . A rare couple . . . Laughter . . . The coming and going of the waiters . . . Jazz filtering through the walls . . . I wanted to recall the fascinations of Africa: underdevelopment, epidemics, misery . . . But these might dirty the roses blooming between Isabelle and myself . . . "No, you're wrong. We are not an extraordinary couple, Isabelle . . . We are the incarnation of provocation . . . That confuses them. You have to understand: for them you live and exist only because of me this evening: because of the downfall that discloses me as black . . . If they'd let go, they would stone us, believe me . . . " — "Come, come, Nara! . . . They're not savages . . . "

Savages! I pursued my astonishment to the very end . . . I drained every conventional restraint without remorse. Then I understood Isabelle's despair: I didn't resemble the image . . . Without taking any precaution, I had eluded nature . . . My nature . . . Isabelle could neither reject me nor spit on her brothers . . . She called upon me, very nicely, to understand that there could be no question of collective guilt, that never had any race . . . I wanted to cover up the body of my hatred to make it into a bed. But she jostled me, clarifying the gift of her sex and the generosity of her feelings. She was broken. But her exhaustion mirrored the hard self-confidence of a truth: Isabelle was the incarnation of Europe, drove me inside herself, convinced that she was able to convert me with her love to the bitter understanding of a revelation in which the plural consideration was to redouble the violence of a suppressed primitivism . . .

Another choice! It was, rather, an abyss, in the face of which the mosquitoes and the heat of the night around me seem like a peaceful garden. What other line should I erase? And besides, it's getting late . . .

II

September 9, 197 . . .

Camara had invited me to dinner in honor of his birthday. Soum insisted that I join them and, in order to help me overcome my hesitation, had promised me emphatically that it would just be the few of us: Camara, his wife, he himself, and I. Rashly, I gave in.

A calm abyss . . . Really . . . Tania, Camara's wife, was very nice: unobtrusive, most attentive, anticipating our every need, filling our glasses regularly, quietly passing the various courses; coquettish and coy in order to get the conversation going again when silence fell. In a moment of utmost euphoria, I told her she looked splendid in her classic, loosely cut dress. She responded with a grimace and, apparently without malice, threw the words "You're drunk" in my direction. She got up and went back to the kitchen. Soum and Camara laughed until they cried.

Humiliated, I had to play the fool to save my face. I held forth on the qualities of her dress of light wool homespun, commented on the grace of the scalloped neckline with its large collar, the studied carelessness of the belt, casually tied around her waist . . . The snub remained and with it the hilarity of my companions. I wanted to stop thinking about it and pretended to enjoy the Irish stew, which to my taste was not sufficiently spicy . . . With a smile on her lips, a glint in her eye, Tania gave me the recipe: "You cook the vegetables in salted water, you brown the meat, cut into cubes, in hot oil together with some minced onions, you season it with salt and pepper, sprinkle it with flour . . . "

I listened politely, my mind elsewhere, wondering how

much longer the show would go on. The heat was all around us, heavy, oppressive . . . All over my body, especially down my back, I felt rivulets of sweat begin their stream downward. The conversation was dying . . . Soum had imprisoned himself in an unusual silence. Was he holding something against me? Not very convincingly, Camara was trying to maintain a false atmosphere of joy, his voice hoarse from the alcohol, his gestures loose and disconnected. Tense and exasperated, I looked Tania in the eyes. They expressed extreme contempt. Fine, I thought, I am a century plant melting in the heat. A corpus of feelings inside a body about to burst . . . I'm not even suffering . . . The transparency of the trap is really rather amusing . . . I should go and sit in a dark corner and look sullen . . . She would come to me . . . "Is something wrong?" — "No, not really . . . My hip hurts . . . " Her nails are scarlet, her filmy dress still is a recrimination . . . "Do you like it?"

I didn't come back to life until we were at the Soleil Rouge. Free from Tania, Camara let loose: as we walked in, he took Soum's hand, began to sing "The International" and to beat the time with his right foot. Immediately a waiter came to silence him . . . Camara pulled him into a devilish dance and made the whole bar laugh. He didn't calm down until the owner showed up. Then Soum led us to a far corner . . . The beer party that it had turned into only stressed Tania's words "You're drunk" . . . But now in the plural, I must insist.

Later on, I tried to redirect our sluggish conversation. I succeeded in extolling the virtues of the symbolism of the Kuba scarifications and wanted to convince Soum. By referring to the myths, I demonstrated that the different designs, traditionally cut into the shoulders of the men, are celestial landscapes; I showed him that the lavish designs the women wear on their abdomens are codes of a knowledge that can open doors to the mastery of the universe. He was smiling . . . I could feel disaster approaching . . .

"Words, words, words, my boy. Beautiful words . . . Among the Dogon this knowledge is buried deep inside learned myths. And that really advances them, doesn't it . . . To know the depths of the heavens and to remain stuck in underdevelopment . . . " I had the impression he didn't want to do me in entirely . . . He seemed to take pity on me: he was going to spare me. Should I convince him? "That's not the point," I said. "It's a question of understanding the wealth of a culture, of learning to draw forth its reasoning . . . " — "Yeah! Reasoning of a cult of difference . . . Now there's a good project for the disenfranchised: attractive masks for the tourists and worship of the word for the ordinary folk . . . "

He was no longer smiling. I was afraid he would, once again as was his habit, go to town against the bourgeoisie; would surrender himself to the ritual splendors of the tropical dictatorship of the proletariat. I knew what panic was: why this desire to share my temptations? Since it proved to be impossible every time . . . I wanted to excuse myself, ashamed to have behaved so improperly. "Certainly. But you know very well that we are something more than mere forces of production . . . " — "What, then, pray tell?"

I was going to have to give in. Find a way out . . . Bitter in the face of my own helplessness . . . The term suited me well. I dreamed of expressing the purity of a monument. The project was stupid, according to Soum. The expression of confusion and distress . . . I needed to alter my course: abandon the jagged pieces of my broken jugs somewhere along a dirt road, take a pickax to construct highways instead . . . Condescendingly, he explained to me the best way in which to pay homage to the African soil: "For about thirty years now, they've been trying to divert our attention. They loudly proclaim the wealth and the complexity of our culture . . . What a joke! When most of us don't even get one decent meal a day. You see, Nara, with Negritude they've taught us that we have something to think about . . . A pastime for rich kids . . . You, who are a historian, you can make the comparison: they would like us all to be specialists in defoliation. Think of the problems of *The Triumph of Henry IV* by Deruet . . . "

It was precisely this last appeal that seemed to reconcile us. I didn't understand his objections. How would our people experience all its desires if, over and above architects and builders, it couldn't have culture enthusiasts who, on occasion, could search for and find the secret upsurges of our traditions . . . As in the case of the painting of the Musée d'Orléans: thanks to the infrared rays, one sees behind the cart pulled by Science, Music, and Art another beach: the lovely female allegories are naked . . . And, underneath that scene, painted over because of Madame de Maintenon's prudishness, one finds the portrait of the first wife of the Duke of Lorraine, Henry IV's sister . . . Shouldn't we accept the past? And how can we express this past if we cannot bring it out into the open, patiently, layer after layer? The extreme rigor and care of the archaeologists have always seemed to me to be a good mirror of my freedom as a Negro. Soum, staring intently, was making fun of me . . . "Nara, don't ever forget this: to be a Negro is nothing exceptional. To be a proletarian, yes. The proletarians are exceptional. Do you understand? That is very important . . . " A screen . . . Then a wall . . . "A solemn moment, this. Long live the proletariat," Camara interrupted.

He smiled at me as if to say: "Nothing matters." Then he put his arm around the shoulders of the young woman sitting next to him. She had joined us at about two in the morning, had picked Camara, and was studying us. Camara called her by name: Marie-Astrid. From the moment she arrived, I had been struck by her gathered red shirt, held taut by her breasts. From then on I was vigilant, waiting for the moment that Camara would dare to undo one or two buttons to kiss her breasts. He was holding her closely. With her right hand she lifted his face, looked at him for a long time, and kissed him on the mouth. Camara tried to nibble on her lips, but seemed stupefied by alcohol and sleepiness. Soum spat on the floor. I thought of a burial. I toyed with the idea of suggesting a walk on the boulevard to him. Together, the two of us would have fought off my dread of the night. But I remained fixed in my seat, my eyes on Marie-Astrid, my mind tormented by Soum's certainties . . . I didn't understand the split he created between the virtue of being a proletarian and the banality of the condition of the Negro.

I didn't go home until the wee hours of the morning. Five or six o'clock? I don't know anymore. Anyway, what does it matter? Soum, who began to reveal himself a little, intrigues me. His plan is cold, perfectly rational, and has, above all, the remarkable power of naming every misfortune, of integrating each one into a gigantic tableau of the salvation of the universe. Soum has faith in a method. He knows its weapons . . . "You should join the Party, Nara. You'll be stronger because you will no longer feel isolated. We can offer you a thinking that is shared, the ardor of a shared brotherhood in struggle, the discipline of long-term action. We, Communists, believe that dialectical materialism . . . "

I thought that I understood him when he left me. He was swerving toward allegory. To tell him at that moment about the course of my Negro anguish would have seemed insulting. He seemed so little concerned with the iron bonds of his race. He was numbed by his faith in the efficiency of a method: what possible weaknesses could he know?

I slept all morning. Was awakened at noon by the landlord, who finally came with a repairman to fix the air-conditioning, so he said. I heard hammer blows, the grinding of steel, cursing. I fled to the shower, where I began to read a detective story. Bits of conversation floated toward me, as absurd as the aftereffects of an illness. "I'm telling you, something isn't right . . . " — "He isn't expensive, you know . . . " — "Their party? I swear, it's pure sorcery . . . " — "What a shame! Did you see the price of a can of sardines?" — "Sure. You can find the best machines at his place." — "And, believe me, that will mean revolution. One really can't feel sorry for him . . . They must have laughed, that's for sure . . . " — "I tell you, it's mice. They would eat through stone . . . "

Worried, I pushed the door open. The worker was gathering up his tools. My landlord, cigarette in mouth, was turning in circles . . . "You will, of course, come back to repair this machine?"

I wanted to know what the story was about the mice. Where were they? The worker shrugged his shoulders fatalistically. "When I get the parts. You know how it is, don't you? No more spare parts. Obviously, if you should find any . . . "

They went away. Once again I thought of the mice. They reminded me of a story. Of a childhood, too. But had I not hoped for oblivion, even though that was just an illusion? "Dr. Sano, you are lying to me: how can one overcome a memory like that?" Words and images don't pair up. They do not match. A hollow resembles a howl. It wasn't the tormented face of my father, but the enormous snout of a rat wrapped in a white sheet . . . I ran, red-hot with terror, into the cold light of dusk. "You see, Dr. Sano, it wasn't simply a flight. But a tornado. My liberation had been rigged: the closet, a wounded face, and then the night that swooped down upon me. Tell me, Dr. Sano, what is there that isn't rigged?"

I'm sure that she was keeping an eye on me. The afternoon suddenly seemed heavy. I was in a rush to leave the apartment. And Aminata came. She was telling me that Salim had obtained an invitation for me to the exhibition of the art of the Kuba at the Musée systématique. She settled down in an easy chair facing the window. Standing behind her, I no longer knew what to do. I had been touched by the gap in the zipper at her belt, which marred her appearance. I looked at her. All I could be was the son. And she the mother. What was she looking for? I took a chair, sat down on her left, somewhat at an angle so that she wouldn't be facing me directly. "You didn't come to the library today . . . "

It was a question. The interrogation. She was smiling. And her shoulders moved along with the turn of her head toward me. Should I ask her what right she had to be requiring an explanation? I didn't have the time. Her look seemed clear, attentive, almost kind. Did I really need to flee from every hand reaching out to me in order to live? "No, I'm tired . . . "

A gate creaked. I was looking for cigarettes. If I can't even hold on to these little habits, then nothing else would give me pleasure any longer . . . "Are you coming to the exhibit?" — "When is it?" — "The opening is at five o'clock

. . . " I tried to make her understand how tired I was. My passion for the Kuba epic had nothing in common with the excitement over the dead symbols of an art opening. This kind of an event, fostered by the commercialism of Europe, is the most perfect example of defilement: life exhibited behind glass. Her face was heavy. Her chest large. Her skin looked soft. How could I tell her? "It's really very kind. But . . . " — "But what?" — Her look hardened. What a preposterous idea to give oneself over to the vitality of others! A bubble of weariness rose in my head. I wanted to describe its contours in detail, got lost inside the embellishments of a dizziness that fogged my view. "I really am exhausted." — "That's why you should come; this will change your outlook, relax you. Come . . . "

Yes, I thought: for my interest in you has its price. Strip yourself and follow me. I will teach you where you'll find what's good for you, will show you how to use your feet, will name your dreams' kindred relationships. She was tender: her look pure, candid. I imagined her with her arms open, ready to take me under her wing, holding her robe widely spread to wrap me up in. Yes, the tepid warmth of a shroud. And Isabelle's panting breath, which scanned my servitude of the summer nights in a little village of Haute-Vienne: "My black love, you are in charge of our desire . . . " I wasn't in the mood. Then she recited Suzanne Allen: "Dearest lover, for a moment you lie next to me, outstretched, like a big X. A knot in the middle. Annoyed. You don't speak, you don't move, your arm is covering your eyes. I tried to soften the cruelty of my avowal. I covered you with kisses. But, susceptive, you were already sliding off the edge of the bed; you were gathering up your men's ways, putting your large foot on the floor, raising yourself high into the useless air, almost as one hangs oneself; you were taking some evasive steps into the room, naked, weakened, disarmed . . . You lit a cigarette. You came back and sat down next to me on the bed, looked at me for a long time with doubt in your eyes, while you exhaled a most distraught cloud of smoke. In my look you sought for the darkness of the end you presumed—quite wrongly—of our affair, or in my disturbed features for some sign of confusion that would have proven my capriciousness. But all you saw was an ambiguous smile, that smile of frustration that often indicates that I have hidden schemes. I let you leave without a word. I was quite sure you would be back."

On the fourth day, I slipped out of bed at five in the morning, slid through the doorway, took the first train, and left the torment of being loved once and for all . . . "I really can't, Aminata. Also, Soum promised me he'd stop by . . ." It was a consolation to hear her answering me, her voice both warm and sad: "Of course, you're right, you poor thing . . . You should rest."—"Yes, I really need it . . ."

Now I could be flexible . . . I was pleased that I had so easily managed to extricate myself from her plans. Again her look was hard. How was I to escape from the snares of this woman? I mimicked a weary smile: "I have bourbon. Would you like some?"—"Oh yes, please. But are you allowed to have any? What does Dr. Sano think of that?"

That was nasty. I blew up: she was invading my life, taking the prerogative of applying brush strokes to my being. As if she alone could be my salvation. "He doesn't think anything of it at all, my good friend . . ." She was offering me a will to live: her own standards, the trap of her own indiscreet watchfulness. I score a point . . . She is interpreting the incongruities of her own game . . . Should I blame her? A star is born and immobilizes me . . . She has a pretty face, that is certain, but her opinions about my vocation do not touch me in the least . . . An ant inside my landscape . . . Another one . . . I saw again the immense termite hills of the southern province where I was born . . . Reddish lumps, lewdly pointing to the heavens, breaking the harmony of the flat savanna. I thought of the termites impregnating the soil with their saliva so as to break it down and cause these little petrified hillocks to bloom forth. By her mere presence, Aminata embodied a threat. And there I was, clumsy, mouthing niceties, offering her my bourbon, as if she were about to introduce me to pure joy. I owed it to myself to pretend to be enjoying her visit, in order to survive, to prevent her nastiness from erupting over me. And it was then that I understood, very physically, the flawlessness of Cioran's words: "It is thus that the familiarization with our disappearance, based on our investment in lassitude, allows us to realize our derangement—our essence—inside our ample flesh . . . "

She shrugged her shoulders and asked me if I was thinking of going to the movies tonight. Again I called upon the lie: that I was expecting Soum. Afraid that she might overstay her welcome, I added: "If he doesn't get here by six, I'm supposed to meet him at Camara's at eight o'clock."—"No," she said gently, "you know very well that you should be resting. I'm taking you home with me for some dinner. You'll be back early . . . "

I was speechless. What pretext could I fabricate to escape from her? Now that I'm reconstructing that day, I'm amazed at her patience: wasn't she, in her eagerness, suffering from my evasions? She seemed determined to force herself upon me as my refuge. All told, was it not better this way? The hidden hatred I was feeling for her was not strong enough to protect myself from her . . . "Thanks, Aminata. Take me with you. Let's go right now. I'll leave word for Soum. He'll come and get me at your place . . . " I surrendered. I thought she felt some real happiness: little sparks of light were dancing inside my head. I was voluntarily entering a cage. Was I so innocent that I didn't understand the meaning of this departure? She was taking me by the hand, was gathering up the shreds of my life, and with a motherly smile she was putting a stop to my last hesitations. She didn't even seem thrilled with her conquest. I was an appealing dog whom she was planning to feed. An ebbing . . . A few silent images . . . So old . . . I'm rehearsing a play. A halo of light . . . In a corner, a mahogany cabinet . . . I'm supposed to deliver a speech . . . But which one? . . . One step . . . into the spotlight . . . I turn to the left. There, a few yards away, is an asphalt road. I'm going to follow it. In it I can see bits of mica shimmering. Ah, the song of my shoes on these broken fragments! I move forward into the music . . . "It is extraordinary . . . Did you know it? This music is really superb . . . And that theme . . . There, there it is again . . . Brilliant, isn't it? He is a genius, Rachmaninoff . . . " I am a miracle: my feet on the road move to the beat of a concerto . . . "Tell me, Nara, why is African music so different . . . "

I turn around. She shakes her blond head. The rain of her hair . . . "Ah! Now there's a question . . . Come, Isabelle . . . we're going for a walk . . . " It is ridiculous . . . I'm in flight . . . She is there . . . The fronts of the buildings accentuate my distress: I really am the center of a storm . . . And I'm walking in the sunset . . . looking innocent . . .

Dusk . . . We are going through the dirty alleys of Krishville: the very oldest, also the most forlorn of this city. She leads me to a place from which there is no escape. And I see my thoughts joining in with my step that sinks into a pool of urine so as to avoid large puddles of putrid water. The risk I ran was inside me. It vanished that evening, simply because of Aminata. We passed in front of a completely empty bar emanating loud music. In the air the strong stale smell of alcohol mingled with the foul stench of the sewers. Little children, their upper bodies bare, were playing soccer at a far end of an alley. We passed around this, tomorrow's young and glorious humanity, with its short, puny legs and distended bellies. A mad king ought to emerge and take possession of this small, decomposing realm. The crowd was there: very young, seated or standing, watching us go by with an odd grimness . . . In a small voice, Aminata said to me: "You're not too tired, are you? We're almost there." — "I'm all right," I said.

Was she offering me relaxation? I was going to pay for it dearly, I feared. I had left everything behind, without regret, without heroics either. Resolutely, she had made me climb a slope. Precisely where she wanted me to go. And I was slipping on the incline, in the most natural way, tormenting myself about the pitiful society that was a witness to my downfall. Never had I looked so intently at the cesspool into which my life was disappearing: scraps of people, huts not even finished but already gray, smells of cooking oil coming from open-air kitchens, drifting among the air currents of sewer gas. And, with every step, the danger of plunging one's foot into this royal shit . . . I admired Aminata's dexterity as she adroitly avoided these threats sleeping on the ground, her head held high, her look riveted on a distance. "Aminata, fifty years from now . . . " She barely turned her head, clearly awaiting the rest of my question. I hesitated at the brute strength of the secret laid bare. She answered: "We shall be very, very old . . . " I wiped my forehead with my hand, worried about the weight of the evidence to be shared. Soum would have understood. In return, he would have proposed the power of his dialectic. And perhaps hope would have replaced my distress. But without faith? "Do you think, Aminata, that this neighbor-

hood could have another face? Look at these children . . . "
—"There now, Nara, we're here. Come . . . "

Two young children, about four and six years old, emerged almost immediately from the house and welcomed us. Quite dark, attractive, eyes sparkling, they were naked . . . "My children. Don't you know them? The older one is Lou. The younger one, Baka . . . I've been married. You did know that? Come, come in . . . "

The living room was large. White dustcovers protected four easy chairs. A table along the wall. Children's clothes all over the floor . . . From a dirty-white ceiling dangled a bare light bulb, which was on . . . A washed-out photograph of Kwame Nkrumah on the wall, right next to the window. Shutters in bad repair clattered in the wind. Just above Nkrumah, in the center of the wall, framed in silver, was a gaudy-colored reproduction of the president and founder of the Rassemblement Populaire de la Révolution, our one and only party, the one now in power. In the air hung an odor of fuel oil, cheap cologne, and indigenous cassava-based alcohol.

I settled into an easy chair, wiped my face, and relaxed. Suddenly, I felt as if I were onstage. Aminata came back with a bottle of beer in one hand, a glass in the other. She was building up and fortifying scaffoldings. I wasn't worrying anymore: this living room protected me against the night, growing darker outside. Here was a place where I could pick up and play out my yearnings and my little dramas without any major consequences. I could let myself go. I took off my jacket, put it next to the artificial flowers on my left. I felt myself revive: hunger rose from my stomach to the top of my head with a rumbling, insistent noise. The streets of Krishville became distant at the horizon, off toward the faraway Indies . . . And I remembered once having told myself: "Paradise lies in desire . . . "

If, at that very moment, Aminata had only known! She was putting a gray tablecloth on the table, and on it she placed a flowerpot with canna lilies. Again, I perceived behind her gestures the hard and conscious expression of a will to belittle. She meant to welcome me, was establishing the framework and the lines of conduct . . . I thought of the vigorous growth of young shrubs. Life arose from ill-known depths as a violent force and took up a place in the sun . . . But what, then, was my expanse? Was I going to survive here? Embarrassed, I decided to let the currents take me along, even if it meant I had to become Aminata's slave. If she could, at least, force me in a more intelligible way! Then I would find a way to pretend resistance, just to save face . . . Pulling a fast one, even symbolically, would give me a good excuse to worry . . . A raised stick can force a dog . . . My head is spinning . . . thinking that, with time, the words we exchange would swallow up my distress . . . In the meantime, here I am, surrounded by debris . . . Twisted streetlights, trees charred by lightning, crates with their bottoms knocked out, and at my feet splashes of mud. I look at her. Her ears are pierced . . .

This was no farce. But a drama. Oh, just a small one . . . The two children, Lou and Baka, were eating in the kitchen. She and I at the table in the dining corner of her small drawing room. In vain, I was looking for the advantage I might take of this tête-à-tête. She was chewing conscientiously, neatly: her eyes half-closed, her lips together tightly . . . Her slightly bulging forehead was shiny in the light. Small beads of perspiration pearled at the base of her nose. I sought to catch her eye and forced her to look at me. "It's very good, Aminata. You're a good cook." — "Really?"

A dead gaze. Had I been mistaken, then, thinking that desire was lurking in her behavior? What else could be confused for the call of a woman? Her smile had vanished, made place for an extreme weariness. I stopped eating: so there wasn't even the illusion of love. I lowered my head. My appetite was gone. And softly, very quietly, the tears came. I could think of nothing else: just to understand a gesture, to name the sign that had led me here in spite of myself.

Aminata had gotten up. She took me to a bedroom. Immense heaviness in my legs, remorse in my heart . . . At my age . . . A fit of weeping! Close myself off? "You'll be able to rest here. You have a table if you want to work . . . Tomorrow I'll get the things you've left over there."

She had kissed me on the forehead. Motherly. Then she withdrew, gently closing the door behind her.

I feared the prison and the condemnation to come . . . She was consecrating me to loneliness tonight . . . In her absence I made my bed. Her only usefulness would have been to secure her willpower against my freedom, unless I've gone off the deep end completely . . . I am her object. I know she'll call upon Dr. Sano if I decide to cry out. If she had any spirit of sacrifice, the meaning of her affection would stink of charity. "A man-eater," Soum said. He warned me a year ago. "She has an instinct for ownership, a feline patience, and the willpower of a bitch in heat . . . Watch out, my boy." I tried to follow the outline of her open thighs in order to imagine her body more literally, to give a name to it, and to destroy it in the ludicrousness of an orgasm that would resemble the bland bursting of a soap bubble . . . All I could do was compensate for my own deficiency: my disgust for a woman's sexual organs was thus inscribed, in an intense inquisition, through my tears of humiliation. A sudden concern for myself. It becomes encrusted. I have become conscious of my body . . . Without any emotion at all . . . No bother . . . I'm going to sleep

. . . Isabelle is watching me. "You're closing the window?"—"Are you cold?"—"Not especially . . . I don't see the connection . . . " It is true. I'm barefooted. I go toward the window, aware only of the contact of my feet with the wood floor. She observes me. Baffled, I wonder what's at stake. When I come . . . That fear . . . Her voice . . . "My darling, oh! my darling . . . " Her arms, her hands, her eyes, her mouth, her fingers around my genitals . . . And above all . . . yes, above all else, her little bird cries . . . The window to be closed becomes terribly important. Becomes a challenge to time. My step grows slower . . . Look at the clock in face of the horror that will explode once I have closed the curtains. My eyes become vacant . . . Embarrassed . . . Impatient . . . "My God, you can be so slow, Nara!" That, they say, is how you break rocks.

Undoubtedly, Sano would answer that I keep up my lack of carnal impulses through pointless worrying. Maybe. But the fact that I scrupulously remember, as I am doing now, this day as long as a lifetime, and that I ask for nothing other than the right to scream, allows me one question: to know the reason why, every single time, only my fear and my heart are condemned to the whipping post.

III

Worked very well today. From the moment the library opened, I delved into the reconstruction of the historical relationship between the Lele and the Kuba. My notes were multiplying. Veritable caresses. Excitement. For hours on end, I was under the clear impression that I was inside a fire. It felt gentle to me. A body that gave me nourishment. Its strength was flowing through me. My communion with it was profound. Ideas came to me, my hand took control of them, and they wrote themselves, as it were, on my index cards. In the course of just minutes I revealed secrets that had been hidden in the depths of centuries: thus I could name the genealogy of kings, thanks to the information I had received four years ago from my research assistants . . . I also rediscovered the meaning of forgotten wars between the Bushoong and the Bieng, between the Ding and the Pyaang.

They used to shed a great deal of blood. Strength was proof of honesty. Its expression the sign of the divine will. In 1634, when the monarch of Bushoong descendency was vanquished by the Pyaang rebels, he stood straight, awaiting destiny. To the slaves kneeling before him, who were begging him to turn away, he said: "God does not die. Sweep up these dead bodies . . . They are in my way . . . " And when he was struck dead in the back by a traitor, he raised his right hand to the heavens in prayer to the Ancestors: "Such is your will . . . " And collapsed.

To take my mind off my card catalogue, around eleven o'clock I skimmed J. Dansine's book *The Ancient Kingdoms of the Kavana*. What a mess! What he writes under the pretense of scientific certainty is truly astonishing. Only in African history can the practice of silence and the art of allusion be seen as evidence of cautiousness. To make Salim laugh, I had a good time substituting the Spanish for the Lele and the Portuguese for the Kuba. This produces an enormously funny text that indicates the level of seriousness of Western scholars experienced in African matters: "The Spanish and the Portuguese are placed under the same heading, not because they have similar political systems, far from it, but because they have a common origin, speak practically the same language, and share a same culture. The traditions of the Spanish, just like those of the Portuguese—at least of the central Portuguese—claim that these peoples go back to a same common origin and are issues of a Woot ancestor . . . "

Salim was beaming. His eyes were laughing with merriment . . . "Go on. Why don't you translate a whole chapter like that. And try (?) to get it published in a European journal. We'll see if they'd dare to accept such approximations . . . "—"Yes," I said. "It is ludicrous . . . Concerning the African, concerning Africa, everything is possible, everything applies. And without any appeal . . . "

What a joke! Because of it I forgot my own discomfort: were these illustrious Africanists, as they call one another, nothing but good souls desperate for some fame? Africa would allow them their dreams . . . All the mystifications as well: " . . . Spanish tradition claims that the Spanish people, presumed to be identical to the French people, were to have come first from the southern part of the territory, then to have gone north quite slowly. But it is possible that they might have come from the West in earlier days. The aristocratic clan . . . would then be a group that descended from the Woot . . . "

"Look, Salim, that is what my mentors say! About Africa. The game I'm presenting is most edifying . . . Now let them tell me that history is a rigorous discipline . . . "

There are surprises that mollify. I wanted to laugh. And I had invented a weapon for myself that became transformed under my very eyes. I had become my own victim: Dansine's sentences beleaguered me. Walls of sand. But stretched out over miles and miles, as far as the eye can see. Salim's face fell. He told me he was sorry . . . "You should destroy . . . No, build . . . Leave it to the Toubab to tell their lies. Since you are no longer victimized, go ahead and write our history."

I was standing in front of his table. He was sitting down. I could see the veins in his bald skull. There were conspicuous spots where they bulged out and faint crisscrossings where the blood pulsated. I told myself that these were probably the centers from which his affection for me started out. He could know my world—for a fact. His protruding eyes pierced the air. I dreamed of inscribing it in brilliant letters with concentric circles of hate: from the first one to the last, as in every initiation ritual, there would be a deepening of the significance of the symbols, those of failure and sacrifice, of death and of life. At the center of the path, a divinity would reveal the parody of the brotherhood: Khepri, the sun-god with the head of a scarab, immortalized inside the tomb of Ramses I, would unveil the mystery of the ecstasy of the king, symbolized in the temple of Seti I in Abydos, which the blinded eye of the lord recognizes in the allegory of the celestial light.

I would have attached no importance whatsoever to this masturbatory exercise in safeguarding my identity had I not been so thoroughly familiar with the obstinate ambition to succeed both of my Western masters and of my co-students. Virgin Africa, without archives recognized by their scholarship, is an ideal terrain for all illicit trade. The discipline I was used to, thanks to their own standards, gave me the right to demand something other than pretty embellishments concerning the civilizations of the oral tradition. A vile qualification! As if there were a single culture in existence not supported surreptitiously by the spoken word! As if the concept of archives should coincide at all times with the specific expressions brought up to date by the short history of Europe.

"Salim, I'll be cruel . . . I would like to be a Negro historian. And that I truly cannot become without being nasty in turn."

"Yes, if you have the grace of martyrdom . . . "

The sadness of his remark puzzled me. I needed a key. I trembled as I saw his veins begin to swell, distorting his skull. It looked like dry soil whose desiccation had just been turned around by a sudden rush of sap . . . "I don't understand, Salim."

He raised his head, looked at me with his jet-black eyes, so striking because of their steady gaze . . . "What I'm saying, Nara, is that martyrdom is not a calling. One takes it on only by force of circumstance . . . You understand?"

Once again his look became glacial. His patience was wearing thin, his advice frustrated me. I wondered if he wasn't abusing his talent in order to win me over to his innermost constraints. Knowledge to him was a Chinese garden: a colonized, tamed, orderly landscape. The flagstones of the path, like the rough side of flesh, correspond to the little islands spread out across the ponds. A discreet order links the lanes to roofed pavilions as it opens up to the mysteries of open-air galleries. Lightweight bridges are symbols: they preside over the rites of passage.

Brick walls, enclosures that are fragile, punctured as they are by windows with flower-covered trellises, are mysterious codes in a universe that is both finite and consecrated to eternity. So I had to follow a lane to reach a mountain mass. Couldn't move a pebble except on very specific conditions. Nor pick a blade of grass except . . . Seeing me play with concepts, he feared for the truth of nature . . . Salim!

His caution nauseated me a little. Scholarship, as I saw it, was memory. I could dig into it, interpret it in my fashion, catch its mistakes if need be, turn it inside out. Hadn't I seen lies, bloated conceits, and glaring self-centeredness there? All in all, with my modest ambition of wanting to record the special effects of the garden, I was worthy of scholarship, I was its servant. I would gladly admit that there was a bias in my proceedings. But it was completely honest. Whatever the disguise or the artificiality of my feelings may have been in the beginning, something was bound to emerge from the results of my quest. And furthermore, hadn't my teachers of old taught me not to be complacent in any way where truth is the first requirement?

The brightness of the courtyard made me breathe again. A breeze. The sun reflecting on the concrete walls. I entered an ocean. It felt warm and good. Engulfed, I felt the rising of the tide. I was going to be swallowed up, pouring with sweat. I thought I could resist the current. No, I wasn't going to drown. Be purified perhaps . . . I felt enriched by a revelation. At my feet, I discovered the bucket I had seen from the reading room a few days ago. It was dirty, full of small holes . . . I burst out laughing.

Aminata had joined me. It must have been noon. Her lunch hour. "You're laughing?"—"As you see. The bucket is full of holes. Look at it . . . " It burned me up when I understood that all I needed to do was to turn my back to forget the whole thing in the most ordinary way. And yet, this bucket in all its blackness represented mandatory life . . . pestered by time. In addition, it had caused me to start laughing . . . "Come, Aminata, I'll explain . . . "

I was filled with joy. Ready for anything: shatter or melt, merge or flow away. In the midday sun, in that little courtyard shimmering with heat, I was the living image of happiness. "Come here, Aminata, I want to hug you, over-whelm you with tenderness. I'm happy, don't you see? I'm happy . . . Give me your hand, let's sing together, do you mind?"

I had taken her arm firmly: "I'm laughing, Aminata. The sun is out . . . I feel good. And then, too, there's this bucket that gives me power . . . It has holes . . . It's a net . . . I feel like keeping it. Will you clean it?"

A symphony. The diffuse sensitivity of white huts. The sad splendor of black squares . . . And my game stopped. She seemed intrigued by my comments: "Is something wrong, Nara?" — "On the contrary, I'm doing very well in-deed. Salim told me that scholarship is a sacred garden. And this bucket is giving me a lesson in nobility. It teaches me how I can laugh again in the sun. And with that I feel like hugging you . . . Don't you understand? I'm happy, Aminata . . . "

That was it: a very profound feeling. Emerged from nothingness, suddenly, with lightning force. It stabilized my mood. I fairly tumbled into open space. As when I was at the shore with Isabelle.

Night was falling. We were lingering, lying in the sand. Stretched out on my back, I was counting the rising stars: "Do you see the stars, Isabelle? They're being born . . . Look . . . If we stay till dawn, we'll be present at their dying . . . " — "Yes, I like that: stars are born, you put it so well

. . . " — "You know, Isabelle, perhaps we, too, are stars . . . "
— "Yes, perhaps . . . "

It was pure peace. Calm. And the night was coming to meet the sea. A light northern wind. Our hands, fingers entwined, were burying themselves in the sand. Our thoughts were the same, and love, she was saying, was making us one. The sound of the sea broke inside my head in fits and starts. She murmured: "I love you, Nara . . . " I could not see her face, or read the look in her eyes. Only our hands, gently squeezing each other, established a bond between our bodies and the sentence thrown out into the night . . . "Thank you for that, Isabelle . . . " The wind was becoming glacial. I was afraid of catching cold. Isabelle's poetry seemed very graceful to me. I could only thank her for allowing me entrance into her illusions. The intangibility of her declaration aroused the usual response in me: submission and gratitude. In her husky voice she recited some poems for me by André Frénaud, about whom she was writing a thesis for her university diploma:

> *I'm seeking a lost smile*
>
> *if it is meant to be mine.*
>
> *It slid into shadows and I came apart*
>
> *trembling like a cloud.*

Flashy words. Her breathing had become short and shallow. Insects were buzzing in the air. And far off in the sky, the hissing of stars. Isabelle was burrowing in sadness, red roses in her mouth. I would have liked to let myself into her dreams.

Very fast, I move among nothing, always

haphazardly, no fearless light to guide my step.

And I await the clearing,

for want of burning bright enough to glow.

She embodied heavenly life . . . It was almost a short-cut to being emotionally moved. She left me far behind. Because I had no light beams, no favors to bestow upon her in return. So, as usual, I was going to slip up and miss the voices of her phantoms and the glow of her ecstasies.

Stars of night

holes of the great

sieve from which

we were thrown . . .

All I had to counter with were some reflexes to this song. For an instant, I picked up the thread of a few anecdotes: my own research dealt with the politics of the acquiring of the Spanish Netherlands by Cardinal Mazarin. Just that morning, I had reread his memorandum of January 20, 1646, addressed to the French plenipotentiaries in Münster. How could I put such drab material on the same line with Isabelle's poetic passion? I understood the rift. And in response, instinctively and without any maliciousness, I decided to fill in the space left by her words. I recited:

"Fifth reason for acquiring the Spanish Netherlands:

the power of France would be feared by all her neighbors, and most particularly by the British, who are by nature jealous of her grandeur . . . "

Laughter, a blasphemous, uncontainable laughter burst out on the deserted beach. I pulled Isabelle up from her bed of sand. Mad with delight, we ran along the sea as the waves of the rising tide splattered against our legs. Isabelle screamed like a maniac and appeared to be having a tremendously good time . . . That night, for the first time, I experienced the insurgency of joy. A subversion that was born from a shifting of expected patterns, expressed in a rare freedom: the overthrow of all barriers . . . "No, Aminata, it isn't a net . . . This bucket is a basket, take a good look. It's old. I'll get in. And you can carry me home in it together with the charcoal. I'll burn for your cooking . . . Do you want to?"

Aminata took me to a restaurant. I was watching myself follow her, like a faithful dog, nose sniffing. In the taxi I felt her naked thigh against my leg. She was lukewarm, pleasantly soft, lightly perspiring all over . . . I cursed my pants, which prevented any direct skin contact with her. I stroke her lightly . . . Insistently . . . She readjusts her skirt. It is lime green. Velvet. Without any awkwardness, I stroke its short, dense fleece . . .

"Aminata, do you know that I have rats at home?" — "Yes, so you told me. Why?" — "They make me think of my father . . . "

There was a kind of thin, bright ring around the huge muzzle that lay languid on the sheets. Its fur was shorn . . . "I don't understand . . . " No, you couldn't possibly . . . In this taxi carrying us off, I'm trying to tell you something about your body. I touch you and dread that you'll back off. No, you let me go ahead . . . Is the softness of velvet similar to that of a rodent's fleece? "You know, Aminata, you are my little mouse . . . "

You invite me to lunch. But I'm sulking. I wandered off the straight path before, in the taxi. I was in an unknown city. Early in the morning. Emaciated street dogs were roaming around, emptying garbage cans. Whole packs of them . . . The street was deserted. As I passed, they raised their heads and looked at me with blazing eyes. Almost like starving jackals. In the silence, my steps sounded like hammer blows. I was frightened. Went into the first doorway. Of a monumental building. A steep staircase. I climbed on up. The walls were covered with red velvet and a smell of urine hung in the air . . . You wake me. And you force me to eat melon with prosciutto. "Actually, I would prefer port with my melon, Aminata . . . But first, tell me why this meal? Who taught you to eat these sort of things, Aminata?"

You dive into your plate. I remember the outside activities around your house this morning, no doubt the same ones as every morning in the life of the people in this neighborhood: women seated around their braziers, looking pensive; children, shabbily dressed, crouched on the ground or sitting on low benches, dunking pieces of bread in their tin mugs. It is breakfast time. They'll be off to school to learn to read and write. And then what? You asked me if I wanted tea. The cup was chipped. Lou and Baka were making a lot of noise. I tried to start a conversation, but to no avail. I asked you: "What are they doing?" — "Who?" — "Well, Lou and Baka . . . "

Again I saw them, smooth and stark naked, with their mischievous eyes, yelling noisily just like this morning . . . "Lou is at school . . . " — "And Baka?" — "At home. Where else would he be?" — "All by himself?" — "Yes, of course. He has his little friends in the neighborhood. He plays . . . "

Mild astonishment: there was my universe. I was redis-covering it as I chewed my melon. A small adult of six, thrown out all by himself into the streets of a dangerous city. A little guy of four, left to his own devices all day long, responsible for his own entertainment . . . "Don't they eat at noon?"—"No. At five. When I get home from work . . . "

The school of life. Not so long ago, you had told me not to ask so many irrelevant questions regarding the requirements of child rearing. So it was more than likely that my scruples bored you. Nevertheless, the way you were spoiling me intimidated me: prosciutto, grilled lamb with zucchini, cheeses . . . It made me feel guilty . . . In and of itself, every moment of my life embodied a certain luxury, so remote from the surrounding wretchedness . . . As of last night, you add to this your colognes, a silk robe, and the pleasure of meals with flowers on the table . . . It is only to justify myself that I re-created that plunge into the sun, experienced in the courtyard of the library. What a fine surrender, in the words of my master, Cioran: "When we have packed the universe tight with sadness, all that is left to us to lighten the spirit is joy, impossible, rare, lightning-swift joy . . . "

We left each other. You returned to the library. I was going to join Soum and Camara at the bar of the Hotel des Touristes. They were at a table with Marie-Astrid and a large, heavy-breasted woman. Camara, worldly now: "Saran Koutima, let me introduce Ahmed Nara to you, a tormented historian . . . Nara, Saran Koutima, trade unionist. And Marie-Astrid you know, I believe."

I made a bow, shook hands, sat down beside Soum. Saran had lush curves of black flesh. An ardent smile on her lips. Hair braided in the Senegalese fashion, pulled back in points. Small, resolute eyes. "Mrs. Kou—"—

"Miss." — "On tour of duty, are you?" — "Yes and no. Just passing through . . . I am studying the working conditions of the woman. In most of our African countries she is not very well protected . . . "

There was a singsong in her speech, a muted excitement in her voice. It matched the kindness that emanated from her and contradicted the hardness in her eyes . . . "Obviously one of Soum's ideas?" She turned back to him as if to ask for help or for permission. He remained unperturbed, busy contemplating the bottom of his coffee cup . . . "I don't mean to irritate you, but it is a woman's initiative." — "Oh really?" — "Does her condition interest you?" — "Somewhat, yes . . . " — "Take a good look around: the housewife in any urban center, what is that? And the woman in the workplace, is that a human being?"

Camara's eyes narrowed. He took Marie-Astrid's hand. They were getting up. Soum was still staring at his coffee, lips apart. The afternoon was cracking . . . An oven . . . Her words came out in an arrangement of tepid puffs . . . She was gesturing, a somber look about her. I said to myself: the woman's condition is a window that overlooks the sea. She and her gestures . . . She was having her day . . . Soum was dozing. I had my eyes riveted on her chest, those enormous breasts . . . An invitation to sleep . . .

Index fingers in the air, her eyes shining, she tells me: "This business is explosive." I rub my nose, I'm convinced . . . She straightens up. I remember Dizzie . . . Behind her, I climb the steps. She seems excited . . . "You're not going to sleep at my place. Think of Isabelle . . . " — "I'm broke. So no cab. It's two in the morning. So the metro isn't running . . . " — "I have only one bed. You'll sleep on the floor, right? The bed is too narrow . . . " — "Tell me, Dizzie, that sounds like the name of a dog . . . where did it come from? I heard a woman call her basset that, on the place des Vosges . . . " — "I'm not a dog . . . " — "Exactly why. I'll sleep between your breasts. And I owe you an apology, right?"

Saran has the same light breathing as Dizzie. All by myself I am an audience. In her enthusiasm, she is rebuilding Africa. Fine, she's right: women are worse off than animals in these bloody countries, objects of exploitation, flesh for sale. And for millennia now, humility and submission have been the keynotes of their existence. I feel free. I feel like having a beer. Very simply. Is Soum dreaming of Saran's breasts? He now has one eye open . . . Passionately, he is making important statements, his eyes dimmed. "Revolution is not the same as hope . . . It is a must . . . Saran, you ought to know that the social relationships of production in the satellite countries of black Africa . . . "

Her look is very quiet, full of admiration . . . Her eyes narrow. He is affirming things to her that I love: the sun rises in the East . . . the Communist party has a secretary-general who is homosexual, which ought not to be allowed . . . She seems heartbroken. I say to myself: Soum is forgetting to tell us where the sun sets. And then there is the moon. It lights the way for the women who, this very night, will go up to the cotton mill . . . Soum has found his self-assurance again, his finest hour: trenchant and decisive words; a cold, pure look in his eyes, and very deliberate gestures . . . Saran is overcome. Her chest is heaving. Palpitations of the heart, a serenade inside her head . . . She bursts out laughing. I listen. Nothing. I see two white, very regular rows of teeth inside her mouth. My thoughts are fixed on Soum. I would like to intervene. She cuts me off: "Negritude, for instance, is pure shit. Take a look at it . . . " Now there's a precise point of view . . . Soum is thinking. He takes a cigarette, looks at it intently, puts it between his lips, and lights it . . . The smoke makes his eyes blink. I'm counting: once, twice . . . He wrinkles his forehead. My illusions shatter . . . "Yes, Saran, you're right . . . Those are the exact words: pure shit . . . And we have to crawl around in it, too . . . "

I order a beer . . . Primly, Saran prefers lemonade. Soum must have a whiskey-soda. He is superb: surrounds himself with eloquent truth. He is a genius, not only in his verbal articulation but also in his behavior. The way he has of straightening his upper body, which gives him the look of a fully inspired master-teacher, that seeming absent-mindedness in his conversation, the clever way he has of diverting attention . . . "And the finest African intellectuals are avoiding the issue . . . Children . . . They no longer know anything at all . . . Lack understanding . . . as they confront a people that's becoming lesser, feeling more and more helpless . . . They see to it . . . " I let go: youth with its eyes wide open and its heart beating, the bearing of conquerors, whip in hand . . . Soum's face twisted. I thought of lending him my hatred . . . I, at least, was a calm wild beast: I don't need my blood heated up in order to survive . . . Soum is getting worked up. He pounds on the marble. Thrashes. Expresses his loathing. His face tense. A question of scholarship. Perplexed, I watch his amorous conquest of her. Let us strip dialectical materialism . . . An onion layer. A second one. A third . . . Saran's pants of unbleached linen . . . How can she be without them? Her look is languid. I'm imagining her, later in the afternoon, offering her silky, warm flesh to Soum . . . I'm going to pull myself onto a balustrade to see what color his pajamas are. And there is Saran, screaming with joy: the yapping of a raped dog . . . "What is absolutely essential, Nara . . . " Well, well . . . I was still there. But it was a burning vision. "Saran, what did you do with my shoes, dammit?" — "And that blasted inquiry; are we going to take care of that now or later?" — "Tell me, what is your idea . . . "

A truck breaks down . . . To gratify myself, I asked you to describe the broken pieces to me . . . You offer me a morning glory . . . In the sky, laden with glorious images, you give me a reason for the abandoned corpses . . . All our arguments put together form an entire world, Isabelle . . . The rumblings of a run-down vehicle turn you on. I make myself read poetry so that I'm able to make love to you . . . A fine state of affairs, Isabelle . . . Trappings . . . "And that steak?"—"We'll cook it . . . Are you hungry? I'm not . . . It's for you . . . "—"Aren't you having any lunch?"— "Once it's after three, I'd just as soon wait for dinner . . . What can you do . . . " From my end, I'm nothing but a mouth . . . Isabelle is watching me, she seems weary. In her look I searched for the signs of a question. Nothing. Barely any amazement at my appetite. Our meeting ground is shrinking . . . Saran's quivering before Soum is trail blazing . . . Perhaps even the beginning of the world . . . That's it: pomposity, snot, sperm, mud, muck . . . Yes, that's it, Isabelle, the creation . . . A case of the clap offered to the sun . . . Ugh!

IV

September 11, 197 . . .

Hours and hours. The impression of an infinite life that unwinds like a thread along the highway. I run after the far-
thest reaches of a great passion, encounter the impudence
of disillusion, and wonder where the fire escape is. "Soum,
I'm going to Marie-Astrid's. I have to see Camara
again." — "So, you just drop me like that?" — "I have to get
back home early. Before dark. I promised Aminata." —
"Are you actually moving in there, Nara?"

Moving in? In front, fish salteries; in back, tons of
bauxite . . . I'm moving in. That's just perfect. His eyes are
dull. I resign myself. "Soum, I don't know what you mean.
Moving in?" — "Come now, don't tell me there's nothing
going on between Aminata and you . . . " I frowned . . .
Obviously, that goes without saying. I got up, looked him
directly in the eye. Saran was brushing dust off her left
arm, giving me a dazzling smile . . . "See you tomorrow,
Soum . . . I am not moving in with Aminata. Believe me . . . "
Avoid any possible scandal . . . I'm conserving my repu-
tation, as Camara puts it. Aminata and I, that would be
turgid . . . Not to speak of the two children . . . Saran's
hand is clammy. I leave the hotel. The asphalt. The bliss of
passersby. Children come and go, stars in their eyes. Cars.
New ones, black, sleek. The stone the hotel was built of is
really pretty unattractive: the color of a wilted rose. It
looks old compared to the flashiness of the American cars.
My steps. I am alone. Enclosed in a sound box: the one I
create by walking. I say to myself, And what if I did move
in with Aminata, what would actually change? Faces.
Sweating. The mouth of a jaded woman. A nose that was

fixed . . . A man's reddened eyes . . . I would even understand it if my life made some sense . . . This trek in the sun. True genius. I meet young women alone . . . They seem to have a reason for living: their swaying hips reconcile me with the universe.

Camara's car. I walk up to the third floor. I knock. Idiotic. What am I looking for here? Soum simply wanted to have free play. I could just as well have gone in any other direction . . . Why go after Marie-Astrid? A whirlwind begins to blow. Sano is a moron: a stepladder to be climbed. I knock again. "Who's there?" — "Nara . . . " — "Who?" — "Nara . . . " — "Just a minute, I was sleeping . . . " Barely a few seconds . . . She opens the door, a cloth tied around her breasts: "I was sleeping." — "Yes, I can tell . . . I apologize . . . And Camara?" — "He just left." — "But his car . . . " — "Oh, it's a long story . . . He took a taxi. He's coming back to get it tonight . . . But, please, Nara, sit down. This is something to celebrate . . . it's your first time at my place!"

Exhausted. A worn armchair. A noisy air conditioner. The fresh air skips on the fringes of Marie-Astrid's foolish whistling. She has disappeared. Five minutes. Ten minutes. A quarter of an hour. A blessing. It gives me the opportunity to catch the flow of fresh air. She comes back in, a bottle of beer in one hand, a glass in the other. I mumble an apology . . . But the taste of beer in this heat . . . I accept. She serves me. I look at my hands: the skin is cracked at the fingers, the nail of my index finger is chipped . . . It looks like a small, dry reed, broken off . . . Marie-Astrid's thin smile carries the strong smell of cheap perfume. It goes to my head. Trenchant. Penetrating. Marie-Astrid is sitting. The light looks blue. I say to myself that she has chosen the best spot: facing the windows. Her eyes are lively, her reflexes quick. She's rescued the bottle of beer that was about to spill. "My God, I'm getting to be so clumsy! Cheers, Nara!"—"Same to you."—"Are we celebrating your affair with Aminata?"—"If you want, but you know . . . " She's amused at my confusion. Ideas, formed like larvae, rise again. I'm going to stir them up. The room fades away. Oh, just a little. The bottom of the slime rapidly reaches my spirit. I brave it . . . Again? I hear laughter. Far off. Provoking. It takes shape: it is a luminous hoop. It comes closer . . . Minuscule tongues of fire. Linked one to the other . . . A beautiful pattern. And the circle is a small universe ready to welcome me . . . Am I going to die? Again laughter bursts out. So close . . . Marie-Astrid seems highly amused . . . "It isn't possible, Nara . . . "—"Yes?"—"What do you take us for? We're not children! Aminata certainly isn't wasting any time . . . "

There are knickknacks in a cupboard, facing me. The barely closed curtains are blue walls. She gets up, goes to the window, looks out over the street. She, too, is wearing a blue skirt. I wonder what role to play. The Kuba, my subject of refuge, would make a good pretext. I can put something acceptable together from that . . . Fill the time . . . She turns around, goes toward a chest of drawers, opens one, takes out a pack of cigarettes. I take inventory of her furniture . . . She comes back to me, offers me a cigarette . . . She is barefoot. Funny little toes . . . They look like stubby, dried-up roots, crooked, lifeless . . . I begin . . . No. It's too crazy to introduce other people to my Kuba muddle, time and again . . . "You know, two years ago she was together with a bank director. I think you know him . . . Baka's father . . . No, I'm wrong . . . Baka's father is someone else: a certain Jean-Michel . . . I don't know his last name. Anyway, the last one was a total loser; yes, a loser despite his wealth . . . And a brute. Jean-Michel wasn't bad to her . . . He never hit her . . . In any case, he was better than her first husband . . . Him I don't know . . . A shop-keeper from her own village . . . "

Her laughter again . . . It's a mania with her, that laughing . . . She undoes the structure of her words that way: everything is displaced, sentences fall apart, disappear, small bubbles lost in the surrounding air. "And now you . . . It's just not possible . . . She must have fetishes to be so successful with men . . . " — "No, it's not the same with me . . . " — "What? Come now! If she wanted to, she'd have men by the dozens . . . What do you think of that? Aren't you jealous? You know, even Salim . . . " — "No, no, it's not the same thing . . . " — "So you're not her man . . . Oh, please! She really is something else, Aminata is." — "Yes, that is true, she really is something . . . "

She guards over me, surrounds me, protects me, indulges me . . . She took me on just like that, without a word. Come. And I followed her. Fetishes? And what else? And even if it were so? I'm quite happy. Far from the rats, trusting, without a care. A child. She feeds me like a mother bird feeds her young. Simple. I accept it and give her my hand as if to a guide. "Is she delicious?" — "To touch or to taste?" — "Tell me, Nara?" — "She has style . . . Fetishes? An old lamp in a corner of her living room with a shade made of crocodile skin. A lovely room, I must say . . . An easy chair . . . A beauty. Knickknacks scattered around in fascinating disarray . . . " — "Are you kidding yourself?" — "No . . . I'm just not controlling myself. It really is cozy at her place . . . We like that." — "You're possessed, my boy; it's all over . . . " And she laughs. Head back, chest forward.

All that's missing, I thought, is a knife. My hand is shaking. I, too, would like to throw my head back, put my feet on this low little table, bare my teeth. And above all:

not burden myself anymore with questions about the curves of her face. Dare to say: "And you, dear girl . . . You've nothing to complain about . . . " It is the act of possessing that intrigues me. She looks for it outside of me. What would Dr. Sano think of that? I shake my head: "Your hands are on the marble, Doctor. They're cold, those hands. And please, don't touch me." — "Don't worry . . . "

The obligatory phrase: don't worry. You're in an airplane and the engine cuts out? Don't worry . . . I was sorry then that I didn't have anything on the tip of my tongue to frighten him . . . The uncertainties of the terrain, the intricacies of the airways, the nervous spasm in my heart . . . illusions, pure and simple, to be cast aside with a sweep of the hand. What self-confidence! He thinks he's capable of naming every single terror that can distort a face! I'll follow him: " . . . Believe me, Dr. Sano, I have an open mind and my feelings are insolent ones: the passion for God isn't killing me, the fire of the dance doesn't burn me, the opening in a woman's dress barely ruffles me. All I worry about, Dr. Sano, are your words. This is a fact . . . I'm sleeping, curled up, happy to be a small, warm ball. The cover is comfortable. Enfolding me. It's a silky (?), heavy skin. I feel it on my bare arms. I have to get up. There is a reason. I no longer know what that is . . . It's odd, Dr. Sano: there are always important problems that ruin my awakenings . . . I have to leave my bed to run off to some dumb appointment or to something else of that nature. A few days later, when I sum up these moments of anxiety, there's no longer a single argument to support the ghastliness of my awakenings . . . Vile, isn't it? Now, there again I have to make a decision: to get up or not to get up. I find a solution: count to ten . . . And exactly at ten I throw the covers off in one fell swoop. The cold forces me to move. And I howl . . . At my feet, in the bed, is a long black snake coiled around itself. He was asleep, happy, surrounded by my warmth. He uncoils and disappears underneath the bed. Do you consider that a normal dream, Dr. Sano?"—"Yes, of course, don't worry . . . " I dream of a discussion in reverse . . . to arrive at avoiding a mixing of the emotions . . . Then would he be able to help me name the object of my emotional turmoil? Perhaps my most ordinary gestures cover up the semiobscurity of my anguish. For instance, entirely change the most insignificant movements of the tongue, stop them, bring them out into the light . . .

" . . . Completely crazy, Marie-Astrid, your nonsense about fetishes."—"Oh, really! Would you like a few?"—"You have any to hand out? No thanks . . . I've got problems enough as it is . . . "—"If you ever change your mind, Nara, you know . . . "—"Yes, of course . . . I can talk to Camara about it . . . "—"Sure, sure . . . Go ahead and tell on me . . . That's your style, isn't it?"—"I'm joking . . . You know, it's really retarded to die of love . . . it's Toubab . . . Now, I myself would rather die of disgust . . . "—"So tell me, Nara, what are you waiting for? Aren't you disgusted enough yet by the rot all around us? Do the princes who govern us inspire you with a yearning to sing, to dance for joy?"

She shivers, her eyes sparkling. She is shifting around in her chair restlessly. Her skirt has crept up slightly, revealing flabby, heavy calves. She's trying to argue a political case. With conviction. She lacks the attorney general's tone that Soum has. It's rather more plebeian: chaste and embittered . . . "They take us for mental defectives . . . Declarations, patriotic speeches. Empty . . . hollow . . . The lie becomes the system . . . " A silent discomfort, an uneasy rage, fever in the voice trying to control itself . . . "You know my feelings regarding politics . . . any and all politics. The carnival of inaugurations, the practice of violence in the name of democracy, corrupt labor unions, dishonesty established in the guise of virtue . . . "

She had closed her eyes for a moment, now opens them again. They are more fiery than before. That's it, the color of hatred. If it were shared, taken over by fifteen people as fired up as Marie-Astrid herself, she would burn this small, stinking town down to the ground. I sense her edginess. She pinches her nose, leans over toward me . . . "Nara, I can't talk as well as Soum. I don't even want to. His words are Band-Aids to the wounds, they hide the misery. We must look the rot straight in the face. You know what's going on: sleeping sickness is decimating the northeastern provinces. For two years now. Cartloads of dead. Do you know what they've done? Send medications? Not even that! There's no money. The few crates of vaccine sent by the Red Cross have disappeared, were diverted, sold off. What they have come up with is extraordinary: a sanitary cordon . . . Good work . . . With soldiers. Just so the doomed know where to wait for death. Those who try to get through are struck down. Very simple. And long live democracy . . . "

It was a nightmare. She was drawing a very precise picture. I knew how bad it was. To listen to her get so excited about it disgruntled me. She couldn't do anything about it. Nor could I. So, were we then condemned to appease each other by exhibiting our helplessness? Camara, who is quick to react, said the other day: "Let's at least suggest that they open some nursing homes. That would be an intelligent way to provoke them." Soum had responded with a contemptuous pout: "That epidemic is nothing. In the Kaokat district there's corn disease. What a pleasure to be able to die of starvation. A gift from a Negro democracy to the inhabitants of Kaokat. They present the peasants with a choice: leave the region or die of hunger. They flock to the cities only to become beggars. Then, in the North, there's the drought. The officials, the district commissioners and company, do some excellent business with their shops there. A glass of water now costs fifteen thousand francs . . . And yet, in principle, this water ought to be free of charge, as it comes from the rivers in the South, flown in by military planes . . . "

As usual, Soum was playing with knowledge and caution: he presented horror as a colony, arranging it in formations according to genre, he named its varieties with clinical precision, pointed out the possible complications with the detachment of a sadistic veterinarian . . . "That's the price we pay for capitalism, kiddies . . . A great misfortune . . . unless you want to explode the whole works. Just think of it: in ten years of independence, the literacy level has dropped thirty-seven points, buying power has dropped five hundred points, the number of unemployed has grown by two million, the mortality rate has increased by twenty-seven percent. Five devaluations, one every two years. Ah, the Negroes . . . Fortunately, we have religion for the populace . . . Handy, isn't it? An enduring miracle . . . Against every evil . . . It makes you forget the always increasing number of children who die of smallpox or the measles. Look at the number of denominations. A new one every day . . . Names out of a dream: the Church of the Ancestors, the Church of the God Revealed by the Prophet Kazouki, the Adoring Apostles of the Nails of the Holy Cross . . . And, if you'd like, I'll establish a Church of the Crossword Puzzle Solvers of the Holy Blood of Jesus . . . All because God consoles, forgives, dries your tears. So then, good people, blessed herd, follow your guides. Into death. No need for nursing homes. The facts speak for themselves . . . We have one nursing-home, an excellent one, efficient too, cut to the measure of our beloved country . . . And that is our one and only party, our powerful and prestigious revolutionary workers' party, for which the entire world envies us . . . "

Marie-Astrid is scandalized, her eyes wet with tears . . . Speaking of fury . . . I know what it can do. The games the unions play as well. So don't try to scare me: what business of mine are our princes? The game has changed: anger instead of laughter. You, the people . . . I, the political one. Oh no! Look at me carefully . . . I am as free to scream as you are . . . But the revolution . . . First of all, they've already robbed us of the word in order merely to cover up the surface of their powers and the enormity of their dissoluteness. And then, let's be serious: you and I against them . . . won't do much good. You with your doe eyes, your wasp waist, your flabby calves . . . And I, with my broken fingernails, my flat feet . . . "Don't you have the confidence that Soum has?" — "No, mine is a desperate one, ruined . . . Like a sponge left out in the sun for months on end, then in the rain. It's decomposing." — "Nara, I'm not sure either that I see a role for me to play in Soum's revolution." — "Now that, my dear girl, is another story. You're not Saran." — "Pig, you pig, you think of nothing else . . . Anyway, that one, with her big ass . . . Nothing to be proud of. But you, you're a pig." — "Please, Marie-Astrid. I am peace loving and modest . . . for a pig . . . " — "Don't tell me you're angry . . . "

No, no. Not over such trivia . . . But it is true, I do not start singing "The International" because there's an epidemic of dysentery in my neighborhood. I am wrong . . . Wrong, objectively speaking . . . When soldiers parade down the street to a marching band, I tremble. Is that fascism? My hatred is gentle. "It shows your halfheartedness,

Nara." — "You think so? I prefer the taste of beer to that of blood . . . And I want everyone to have a glass of cold beer when it's hot . . . " — "That's symptomatic, my dear . . . " — "Of a shameful disease?" — "I'm afraid so."

It's getting late. Almost six o'clock. I need to go home, Marie-Astrid. "Yes, you're right, they suspect I suffer from romanticism . . . " — "With Aminata, you pig, you're forgetting the revolution."

Once again, her vibrant, clear laughter, her mocking look. She was frowning. Her hand . . . And then there was the tepid air, barking, a dog; a car hurrying down the street.

And I found you again, Aminata. Your face tense in the setting sun. Your hands feverishly busy. My head is turning a little. The alcohol, no doubt. A bitter smile. I am your throng. The night grows deeper. I am rooted in your easy chair. You come and go without saying a word. There's a lump in my throat. I scratch my right ear. My nails seem really dirty. Are you looking at them? I'm ashamed and hide them inside the palm of my hand . . . You turn on the lights. There is this lump traveling between my throat and my chest. Should I talk to you . . . Declare myself guilty . . . Are you sulking? I must have done something wrong. When I left the restaurant this afternoon? "Aren't the children here tonight?" — "They're at my mother's, always on Friday evening." — "What about school?" — "Tomorrow is Saturday." — "Saturday?" — "There's no school on Saturdays . . . "

I feel richly embued with Kuba traditions: the creation of the world, the enthronement of the first monarch, the rivalries at court. My imagination isn't worth a dime. I watch myself asking: "Aminata, shall I tell you the story of the Kuba Kings?" Ludicrous. I have an empty basket instead of a brain. "Are you angry?" She comes closer, pulls up a chair, sits down. Heavily. Odd . . . At that very moment I hear Marie-Astrid's insult again: " . . . that one with her big ass . . . " Does Saran sometimes fall heavily into her chair that way? "I was worried. You said you'd be here around five . . . " She's keeping track. Her look is calm. Elbows on her knees, head between her hands, eyes interrogating me. You are making judgments. I didn't keep my promise. So what . . . "I left the library earlier just to wait for you . . . "

It spurts out: "Forgive me, I was with Marie-Astrid. She was very charming." — "Is she marrying Camara?" — "Is she?" — The rain begins to fall. A cloudburst. The air is getting fresher. You shrug your shoulders . . . "It seems that Camara is taking her as a second wife . . . " — "So I gather. But she'd make more of a disciple of Soum's, Aminata." — "So would you, no? At least that's what they say . . . " — "Not yet. I'm an easy touch, that's all. Misery gets me upset. And they do know how to talk about that in the Communist party . . . "

Was that really all? I pushed a box of matches around that lay in front of me. I really wanted to know. With true mystic fervor. I felt myself above the eternal promises . . . Or below . . . Or next to . . . Doesn't matter. "Promise me you'll always love me . . . " — "You do love me, don't you?" — "As what?"

No, really. Thanks a lot. The chiaroscuro of the dusk suddenly became much darker. Aminata went back to her mechanical gestures: draw the curtains, close the doors, turn a light on here, turn one off there . . . The box of matches began to occupy the whole table: in this empty space, a minuscule and fantastic object. With a yellow belly, decorated by a butterfly; a crossbreed one might say: the beautiful, deep, and bright wings of the peacock butterfly, the dense, fat body of the *Agria narcissus,* the firm, slightly curved antennae of the *Terracolius annae.* Safety matches . . . Made in Tsingtao, China . . . The back as well as the sides are midnight blue; the edges cardinal red. These safety matches have, all of a sudden, become tremendously important. Fire . . . The butterfly will burn up in it . . . Just one of these little sticks and it's an inferno. One enormous flame . . . This house, the whole city, the savanna, the forest, this whole wretched country . . . Purification by fire, one explosion, and a new beginning in a new atmosphere on an earth nurtured by ashes . . . "Aminata, tell me something: at the time of the brushfires during the dry season . . . what happens to the butterflies?" — "The butterflies? . . . "

There are rings under her eyes, as if she had a hangover. Sloping shoulders, sagging breasts, flat belly . . . Well preserved despite her two pregnancies. "I don't understand a thing, Aminata . . . Look at this lovely butterfly, belly up on the matchbox. I always thought that butterflies flee from fire . . . death . . . Do you understand this?"

All in all, is this not a ghastly symbol? If Soum could interpret this! I have a strong urge to go and get him. Show him that the revolution is right here . . . A simple matchstick. "Do you have a record player, Aminata? Put on something beautiful . . . " — "Don't you have anything? The radio then . . . If you want . . . "

I got up to go to the window just to stretch my legs. Feel them come to life. All the lights are on . . . "Yes, I'd love a drink, a small one . . . No, no preference really. No, really. Anything you have. Something that burns as it goes down. I'm a drunkard, can you imagine. That's what Tania says. You don't know her? . . . Camara's first wife . . . "

I returned to the tepid warmth of the easy chair . . . Then the effects of the banana liquor. As usual, my voice gets hoarse . . . The limit. Aminata, an exquisite child lost in a despicable motherhood . . . Prophesy? The frenzy of desire glides through my body . . . I curl up and flow inside the torpor of the night, my thoughts muddy . . . You are a priestess, Aminata. Locked up tonight inside your chapel, it is I whom you must sacrifice. A shutter rattles. The heavy scent of liquor in the air. Just one match and the fire set to Rome by Nero would be no more than a pleasant fantasy . . . Aminata, you're celebrating a depraved religious service: you wring your hands, your eyes are bulging, and your tongue, a scarlet flame between the brilliant white of your teeth, seems of a hellish cruelty. "You see, Aminata, one match would be sufficient . . . " — "Yes?" — "I tell you, just one little matchstick . . . No more scandals, no more peculiarities of our princes . . . Do you know Caligula?" — "Yes?" — "A licentious prince. Long ago . . . in Rome. He resembles ours in every way . . . He had a marble stable built, with an ivory crib, purple horse cloths, halters decorated with precious stones . . . all for his horse. This is a historic fact, believe me. A horse . . . And this imperial horse had a palace, domestic servants, and guardians. So, now you understand the power of a match! As opposed to Soum's golden words . . . " — "You want to destroy everything, Nara? You too? Will you rebuild it all, as well?" — "First a matchstick. So that all rancor, injustice, growing anxieties go up in flames. What I dream of, Aminata, is doing ring-around-the-rosy around a burning palace . . . "

It's true, joy is there, right in that little box. I feel happy. Sano had understood absolutely nothing with his airs of unrecognized pontiff. "The drawings would be better if the yellow was clearer . . . " — "What do you know about it, Dr. Sano?" — "Nothing . . . Not much, at least. But yellow stands for joy. That's what you told me." — "I,

Nara, told you that?" — "I don't exactly know anymore. Work with happy colors."

Of course, there's the yellow against which the butterfly's fat little belly shows. But joy, my kind of joy, lies in the promise of a match. "Does promise have a color?" — "Hope, Nara, is green; sadness is white or black, depending on whether you're poor or rich. But promise . . . " — "You see, Aminata . . . " — "What?" — "Nothing. Excuse me." It doesn't matter at all. Your look, Aminata . . . Somber in this light. Are you playing mother? I'm ashamed of the agitation inside of me. A snake . . . The wood of this little table is coming apart. Light grooves filled with a blackish material. I am fascinated . . . "Aminata, just one match would suffice to clean it all up . . . May I do it tomorrow? That won't bother you?" To feel useful at last.

I question myself: what meaning should I give to all these adornments that I fuss over? Remember: the plans suppressed even before I entered university. Note: the inanity of freedom in the face of the powerful constraints of one's milieu. And there I am, smack in the middle of the trap, dazed by the colors of the very trap that holds me prisoner. The exhaustion of the mind as that of the heart would be a place where life devours itself. Develop Cioran's phrase: "A civilization begins to decay from the very moment that life becomes its only obsession."

V

Of course, nothing is certain. Absolutely nothing. "My hair's standing straight up in the air," she says. "I look like a drowned cat." — "Oh, it looks fine, don't give it a second thought."

And I turn the page. Another one. A series. A hallway. It has to be possible to get to the end of this whole business. "Yeah, of course, that's for sure . . . It's not easy." I tear myself away. She's talking. Tania screams: "He's unforgivable, Camara is. To do that to me . . . to me . . . He's an absolute bastard." The words clatter down. Unmoored barges. Excludes herself: "Men, they're all the same . . . Bastards . . . let's not get into it . . . Monsters, every last one of them . . . " Her voice breaks. Disconnected gestures. Her face wet with tears. Swollen eyelids. Soum is calmly chatting, looking unperturbed. I tell myself we're falling apart. A marriage of broken belongings. A turned-over sofa. A photo album amidst the fragmented dishes. All of that is pretty pathetic. "No. He can't do that to me. I didn't just arrive from the village, a newcomer. Well, he's going to find out . . . "

I put a genealogy together. Salim says to Aminata: "That's what administration is all about, goes after the common people because of the way they use their time . . . " She answers: "It's a question of efficiency . . . " A voice in midair: "It's magnificent . . . " The world lights up. Lightning in full sunlight! You should see it. Only in Africa are such miracles possible. "Lightning, thunder, eighty-eight degrees. Never saw that before in my life."

A determined face. Sad eyes. Chubby cheeks. Not a wrinkle. Greasy, well nourished, plastered-down hair. "I swear, products for American blacks . . . " — "What does it matter?" — "Nothing, actually . . . But to have sunk that low!" — "Oh, no! Never . . . " A smile in the muck. He's glad to be alive. I've discovered a happy African, good Lord . . . But what a mug! He's reading the *Encyclopaedia Universalis*.

"Listen, Aminata, it's awful . . . Do you see what he's doing, that guy?" — "The same thing you're doing, you know." — "Excuse me?" — "What else would he be doing in a library?" Fine. I've found *The Secret Bible of the Blacks* by Prince Birinda:

> *Dewdrops, the breath of* Mukuku
> Kandja *spread throughout the night;*
> Dintsouna *was born from this, as it*
> *mingled with the torrents of blood*
> *and milk that issued forth from the*
> *breasts of the Princess, condensed*
> *into small groups of living atoms and*
> *swam into the night, like salt into the*
> *water of the ocean . . .*

He is wearing heavy shoes, enormous weights . . . Something between a boot and a normal shoe and yet something else . . .

> *The water is like the night, the*

intangible form of Mukuku Kandja;
the salt is as the crystallization of his
breath, whose every particle is a
burgeoning soul . . .

A Terylene suit . . . His legs are crossed underneath the table, the crease in his trousers very visible. Aminata is there again. She whispers: "Holy Mother, did you look at his hands? The jewelry . . . it's gold. Do you think it's real gold?"—"Oh, you know . . . gold or imitation, it's all the same on hands like his . . ."

Isabelle loved beautiful things: jewelry, scarves, hats . . . They stand for life, showing one aspect of the feminine whirlwind . . . The other side of sorrow and poverty.

This breath is sperm blown out
across the Night, like a protoplasm
whose every call is a potential being
ready to germinate . . .

She is as black as the Night, the princess of the Day. Humiliated, on her knees, her legs twisted in pain. Helpless fury in her eyes.

Thick yellow dross in the middle of a curve. The wall is somewhat rounded. A warm trough. That's what the breast is. It should be a nice place to work. A large room, fully carpeted in white, lush armchairs flanked by gigantic ivory ashtrays. A circular hall. A small living room. Luxury becomes the sign of respectability. "My grandmother doesn't speak French and I'm ashamed of that." — "Do you really think it's that important to speak French?" — "My wife . . . the first one, that is . . . I have three wives and soon maybe four, can't read or write . . . " — "That's inconvenient . . . " — "So you see . . . I'm thinking of having her take private lessons . . . "

Noiseless footsteps. The absurdity of a setting becomes trivial. In the final analysis, I am to be pitied. If I had the means, I would undoubtedly have paid more attention to appearances. "Just think . . . Driving a Mercedes and not knowing how to write . . . " — "Especially not understanding a word of French . . . " — "Just like the wife of the vice president of the National Assembly, it really is scandalous, I tell you . . . "

A majestic lion covers the entire wall. Madness . . . Not even. A requirement of militancy (?) in the service of the party. Thus it is that one becomes accustomed to living with wild beasts. Totems. Soum laughs those things off too easily: once he suggested to a circle of friends that this symbol be replaced by a spider.

The landing reverberates. Isabelle gets out of bed. A transparent nightgown. A lit cigarette in her hand. The halo of the bedside lamp is a concerto. I stroke a heavy eyelid with my finger. Her nightgown is a pale-colored nylon . . . A ghost with long blond hair . . . She has come back, sits down on the bed. A nervous amazon . . . I feel panic rising . . . I detest these interminable explanations where everything must be risked while you are in a state between dreaming and sleeping. " . . . Isabelle, are you sick?" — "Why do you ask?" — "It's three o'clock in the morning . . . " — "Yes, the hour of determination . . . I feel like a wreck . . . " — "Try to get some sleep . . . "

With the oracle asleep, I pray for the appeasement of my worries . . . The crises of conscience after midnight take on an aura of provocative magnificence. The staring eye, the closed face, the hard mouth, the cold hand. "Nara, you know, every single time I come back to you . . . Every time . . . " — "Is that a question of philosophy?" — "No, it's my understanding of love . . . the discovery of a body . . . yours, Nara . . . " — "Isabelle, at three in the morning!" — "I make up for it . . . Are there set hours for this?" — "I'm going to leave you if you keep this up . . . Dive back deep into my sleep . . . " — "You are my totem . . . " — "I'm not an animal, Isabelle . . . You wanted a Negro as a cure for the barrenness in your life . . . I'm delighted to participate in your follies . . . " — "So?" — "I'm sleeping . . . " — "You're lying, you creep . . . " — "Am I?" Squeezed dry, I stretch out on broken branches. The night is fading . . . I am no more than a black symbol wrapped in white sheets. A totem. " . . . Isabelle, you've reached a point where you might just as well replace me with a dog . . . " — "Pig . . . " — "No, a dog . . . I said a dog, you hear . . . "

A gentle sob. I feel as if I'm swimming against the tide. The ticking of the clock. A distant mewing of a cat. An idea, undoubtedly. Or rather, a feeling. But what would the tide's direction be? Salim is writing, his head bent slightly. Aminata, a pile of books in front of her, is making out index cards. Her bare legs underneath the table are the most lovely legs I've ever seen. The tide? And what if it were a tie instead, a knot? The dictionary defines it: that which tightens by itself when pulled. Thus, a noose . . .

Note: interject here the duplicity I've lived through with Sano? Important in any event: for two years now the constant theme of certain questions of mine: "I think I despise you, Dr. Sano; but I do like to talk with you . . . " —

"Why?" — "Because . . . " — "Yes?" — "You make me lose my self-respect . . . And I enjoy that . . . " Then the shame . . . He was looking at me, impassive. The windowpanes were steamed up. All of a sudden. With his hands in the pockets of his white coat, he really looked like a doctor, Sano did. With his glasses in gilded frames. In my chair, my back straight, my mind exhausted from having reached these limits . . . It was a surprise to feel my body bend with the inflections of my words. To feel the impurity twist me on the inside . . . The disposition of an atrocious hunger.

I had a sandwich and a banana for lunch at the small café on the corner of the rue des Sékétés and the avenue de Rouen. It was crowded. The atmosphere of a village celebration. A smell of people. One on top of the other. Salim's knee against my thigh. Aminata, opposite me, peeling an egg . . . She is cleaning it very neatly . . . Her eyes are attentive as she works with very precise movements of her nails. Long and clean. Whereas mine, oh God! I pull my thigh back. Nonchalantly . . . Not to bother Salim, who, seemingly, sees nothing wrong in his knee being implanted in my flesh . . .

Next to our table, a fat woman sweating blood, and three men. "Completely crazy, this new law . . . No really, what do they think? Suppressing the right to strike with a law . . . " — "You could see it coming . . . It can't go on . . ." — "So, you guys, you're going to let them do it to you?" — "Quiet, woman . . . It concerns black people . . . Among the Toubab it would already have been a war . . ." — "Don't overdo it . . . Have you lived with them, the Toubab? You should have stayed there, Daddy-o . . ." — "Yes, three more beers . . . And very cold, please . . . " — "And then the boss who just bought himself a brand-new car . . . A shiny new Mercury . . . When he drives up in it, he almost bursts with pride ... So now he has three of them ... With his black BMW and the Mercedes ... You should see him ... Well, that's how it goes ... " — "I don't want any more bread ... Who wants bananas or eggs?"

Once more Salim's leg against mine. Lukewarm. Almost insistent ... I look him straight in the eye. Nothing ... He carefully undresses a banana, his lips moist in expectation. Aminata, for me, has turned into the silent word. Her hair wild, her mouth loose, she is an adjective come to life. Salim piles up dirty dishes, wipes his face with a minuscule red handkerchief. I would love to order a beer but dare not. Aminata generously supplies us with orangeade. She smells of sulfur and palm scent ... A spacious sweep, scored by waterways, extends the table ... It cuts Aminata in two at the level of her navel. Her bust cuts across a bald hillock and a spring ... An optical illusion? As sharp as this? Bright colors: burned soil around the mountain, dead leaves decomposing, gray and white pebbles around the spring ... And then the whiffs of a foreign life, an everyday life: the humid loam, the musty grass, the buzzing of insects, the noisy ecstasy of the waters' madness ... And all I have is this setting in which to dream of a displacement at the end of a pitiful little lunch ... Aminata slips two peanuts into her mouth, her breasts sway ... Her moving jaws cause an uproar: the air howls, the scenery of the water's source is cut through with death rattles ... Sackcloth and ashes ... Salim has pulled his knee back. Suddenly, his common sense wears me out. Now here's a man without desire.

Old age, death, whatever. But long live desire. In Salim all is empty. Age has already cleansed the woodwork, erased the solid parts ... Everything has been equalized, rubbed down, readied for the coffin ... "Isabelle, listen to Cioran ... He is wonderful: 'All that I know I learned at the school for girls' is what he ought to cry out, the thinker who accepts everything, rejects everything, when, following their example, his specialty has become the weary smile, when people are only customers to him, and the world's sidewalks are only the marketplace where he sells his bitterness as his female companions sell their bodies . . . " — "Is he crazy? Who is he, anyway?" — "A wise man such as the West no longer produces . . . " — "So that's your kind of mentor . . . I must say! For a historian!" — "What?" — "The body reduced to nothing other than an object of despair . . . That doesn't make it, does it? You are working too hard, you know? That philosophy isn't worth beans . . . " — "What do you suggest?" — "Nothing, my friend. Nothing besides my wish to live, to laugh in the sun, to burst with joy, to die sated with pleasure and happiness." — "Desire, you say . . . Nothing but desire . . . " — "That's what it's all about . . . Isn't that rather African . . . "

This blonde, always with the same old story . . . A philosophy of mirth to counteract the anguish of being. To use Africa as a refuge is amusing. Obviously, she could bring me hundreds of scholarly works to substantiate doing so . . . Entire libraries . . . Africa dancing . . . The Africa of emotions, of desire . . . The unleashing of the senses in the image of intertwining lianas and the branches of a tropical forest. Green. Debauchery, like the ecstasy from hashish, is green. A tanager has conversations with a nightingale in the dense foliage of trees . . . Green lizards play hide-and-seek with puff adders in the underbrush. Along the swamps, overripe fruits are sweating gold and vermilion: pineapples, mangoes, papayas . . . In the dusk, closing in around the forest, the rhythm of drums covers the buzzing of the insects and proclaims the glory of all carnality: on open squares encircled by mud huts are naked men, firm-breasted women, mothers with pendulous breasts, all beating time with their feet and their hands, hips swaying in rhythm, their bodies dripping sweat . . . the fascination and the thrill of unmentionable yearnings . . . "If that's what Africa is, Isabelle . . . " — "I didn't say that's all it is . . . " — "Your Africa comes straight out of a Tarzan movie . . . " — "Oh, Nara, you're impossible . . . Are all blacks as supersensitive as you are?"

Her wide and silent eyes stare at me, challenge me . . . Defiance . . . You, Aminata, don't have this broken voice when you answer me, nor this face, hard as a rock, that makes me want to start a scene . . . You study me with your calm look, your shiny teeth, ready to bring me into your loving care. You have the eyes of a goddess. The tepid warmth in my loins makes me weak. How can Salim possibly dismiss you just like that? "Do you hear what they're saying, Nara?" Laughing behind my back. Voices, loud ones, in the back of the café, to the left . . . "No, what are they talking about?" — "Just listen . . . " My heart shrinks. Salim's patronizing smile. A man's voice: " . . . I swear to you it's true . . . five hundred million francs for the purchase of spare parts for the ships and the railroad cars of the Maritime Company . . . Spare parts . . . No way! . . . They're eating up all our savings. And that's not all. What the hell are you laughing at me for? I'm not lying! It's in the papers. They've also borrowed eight hundred and fifty million dollars to start a police academy. Just wonderful . . . " — "But where's all that money going? For ten years now we've been getting into debt with the Toubab . . . " — "Exactly. You ought to check the prices in the market. All they do is go up, up, up. And our wages don't budge . . . " — "I tell you, that's democracy for you . . . " I'm back at the table, closing off my ears. "It isn't funny . . . What's so special? It was in yesterday's paper . . . " He gives a little cough. Looking irritated he turns his eyes away. "Just before, the wife was saying they ought to arrest them all, lock them up and force them to eat all that dough in one day . . . " He clears his throat, cracks his left thumb with his right hand, goes on: "Until they're dead . . . It's a quaint thought, isn't it?"

Aminata alone, abandoned, absent . . . She's following the movements in the room. I would like to know what she thinks of all this. Her little crocodile purse is on the table. Her hands folded, as if in prayer, on the table. I admire you . . . The sound of a small bell. I look at the time. Aminata is already ahead of me . . . "I think it's time."

All afternoon I had parrot feathers at my disposal, leopard skins and hatchets in a complicated arrangement so that I could reconstruct the geographic circuit of the pact of reconciliation "through woman," signed between two rival nineteenth-century princes. Most of the Western historians have generally avoided taking daily life into consideration, even if it might have added clarifications useful to the history of the institutions. Some research I did in earlier days, when I spent more than thirty-five months with two Kuba, gave me the opportunity to record the oral tradition for hours on end: the history of various institutions, the knowledge of the pleiad, the moon, the stars, the art of transferring illnesses, the many techniques used by the ancestors for major works of construction and their meaning, the symbolism of different kinds of enclosures and the various first fruits, the labyrinths of divination through the use of purslane, calabash, or simply the hand.

An unfamiliar library with whose organization of treasures I'm not at all sure I am perfectly familiar. For weeks on end, I copied the story of the rites of reconciliation, the primary one of which is the one "through woman," which can be found in several cultures, particularly among the Luba: it sets earth power in motion in order to seal a durable pact. The two princes, convinced of the urgency of a reconciliation, bring together sufficient goods by means of which to purchase a woman who does not belong to either of their clans. Following the same procedure, they obtain a dog. On the appointed day, they go to the right-hand shore of a river, each one accompanied by his most trusted men. The beach has been prepared to welcome a new freedom: a dike has been constructed to curb the water and slowly guide it into two holes dug in the earth. The woman, brought there earlier, lies in one of them, all four of her limbs broken; in front of her, in the other hole, the dog, similarly mutilated, howls with pain. In ceremonial costume, traditional headdress on, leopard skin over their shoulders, hatchet in hand, the two enemy princes face each other, flanked by the holes in which the victims lie kicking. The attendants of both monarchs stand around them, in silent contemplation . . . And that is the horror required by the fate of a reconciliation . . . The funeral begins . . . First sprigs of dried grass, then large stones, finally fists full of soil . . . At this point, only the woman's bare torso is still exposed; and only the snout of the dog . . . I hear her screaming, cursing her own people, imploring . . . The dog howls at his approaching death . . . Heads bow down to the altar . . . The two princes have taken a step toward the sacrificial victims . . . They take turns kneeling before the woman and giving her a bit of cool water to drink directly from the calabash . . . "Woman from Nika, woman from a faraway place . . . I take you as witness before those present here, my men and those of my brother . . . You are about to die and to become the eternal safeguard of our reconciliation . . . If just one of these men here united, just one of the members of his family, just a single child of our progeny breaks

the bonds of our pact today, pursue and punish him . . .
This dog will accompany you . . . He is bound to you for-
ever and will serve you in reestablishing the peace sworn
and sealed on this day . . . Foreign woman, be our protec-
tion . . . "

Once the litany has been recited by each prince in
turn, the crowd applauds. The two leaders throw themselves into each other's arms. The water of the river begins
to rise . . . The two reconciled ethnic groups have gone
away. They will meet again at the intersection of two
roads. There, a pyre is erected. The royal leopard skins are
thrown onto it . . . A goat and a dog are sacrificed and
shared for the evening meal . . . And the two clans, united
at last, will guard the fire of the future until dawn.

Salim's head is tilted backwards as if he were asleep.
Aminata has her nose in her index cards . . . The harshness
of Africa . . . The iron laws . . . I understand that the West
made attempts to impugn her. But only to establish the
echoes of the Me through garrulous symbols. "You can't
know how demanding Africa is, Isabelle." — "That's aw-
fully important to you, isn't it?" — "To tell you the truth, I
don't know . . . I really don't . . . I wonder if I don't just
treat it as a game much of the time." — "Nara . . . I don't
understand. For me the important thing is to be me. To be
a European doesn't mean just belonging to a flag." —
"You've never been hurt the way . . . " — "You're overdra-
matizing, Nara. You wear your African identity like martyrdom . . . It makes me think. I would feel contempt for
you if I joined you in your game." — "The difference, Isabelle, the difference is that Europe is, before anything else,
an idea, a legal institution . . . while Africa . . . " —
"Yes?" — "Africa is perhaps primarily a body, a multiple
existence . . . I'm not putting it very well . . . "

We are on a bench in the jardin du Luxembourg, with our books. Between ten and eleven in the morning. She has a seminar at eleven. I had gone there with her, having nothing special to do. All I have is one course this afternoon from three to five. It is fall. The leaves on the trees are beginning to turn brown. Here and there, as far as the eye can see, pink piles of dead leaves. Three steps from our bench, a black laborer at work. I am ashamed to be here, my arm around Isabelle. Furthermore, it is no longer she . . . I am thinking: "this white girl." My attitude has taken a patronizing turn that allows me to make her nameless. Does he think that "I'm having a good time with this fast chick"? That's it, the scraping of his rake . . . Like a fork cleaning the surface of my open skull for hours on end . . . I am ashamed to be here with Isabelle . . .

"Isa, to be African is in the first place to be conscious of the fact that one is a thing . . . to others." — "It's not only the Africans, Nara, who have the privilege of being made into an object . . . How about women?" — "Isn't that the name of a paper?" — "Quite right. The paper is called *How about People?* . . . I like it when you make fun . . . Both the rights of women and of the people are dismal." — "It's different with the Negroes. For centuries now, without any exception . . . Remember, Isa . . . It was you who found a motto for the MLF[4] in Frénaud: *I denounce my life and remain here, out of mental distress or out of spite . . .* " — "Wouldn't that same motto do for the Africans?" — "Why don't you ever say Negroes?" — "Oh that! You know perfectly well I'm afraid I might hurt you. You can see for yourself how you take these things . . . "

4. Mouvement de la libération des femmes (women's liberation movement). — Trans.

Indeed. I dreamed of removing barbs and prejudices. She heard me speak my piece from her own corner of freedom. To begin with, we should have agreed beforehand on the kinds of parentheses . . . That's only normal . . . Why then did she assume the right to determine both form and content? "Isabelle, it's always the same with us . . . permanent misunderstanding. Europe and Africa . . . between you and me . . . " — "So, if I understand you correctly . . . Love between us isn't possible . . . " — "No, that's not it. What I am wondering is rather under what conditions it would be possible . . . You with your mind for subtleties would appreciate this, I suspect . . . I repeat: under what conditions would it be not thinkable but possible . . . "

Noisy sobbing, the exacerbation of a reddened nose had made me wild and led me to conjectures about the ego . . . and to racial prejudices. Wasn't it idiotic?

My commentary on the rites of reconciliation caused me to make similar mistakes. As then, with Isabelle, in the exile of a belated autumn. I promise myself to follow patiently along the the water's edge as this day ends. Aminata's face shines with fatigue and sweat. Lead her to the cool of the water's spring. A kind intention ruined when just barely uttered: Soum, Camara, and Marie-Astrid dropped in at the library with a great deal of fanfare. Without embarrassment, without any regard for the proper gentleman . . . Marie-Astrid was nasty. In a loud voice: "Aminata, it's simply incredible . . . To have such a creature before your very eyes . . . Did you see those high heels . . . Doesn't it make you want to throw up?" Soum, very much the tribal chief: "Come children, we're all going to the airport to see Saran off. Afterwards, I'm inviting everyone to dinner, and the party can begin . . . Let's go . . . " Salim, the paragon of bureaucratic order, threw us out without any further ado, his hands trembling with rage . . .

A door slams. The curtain falls. An engine throbs. The flood of pedestrians in Krishville. Camara at the wheel of his old jalopy. Saran, regal in her wide boubou, at his right. The four of us in the backseat. From left to right: Soum, Marie-Astrid, Aminata, and me. Close together. In friendship. Our warmth, I am convinced, gives rise to inadmissible longings. To cover up any other possible results, easy laughter spreads a sense of artificial cohesion. A gust of hypocritical affection loosens gestures and inappropriate words. Marie-Astrid's voice has the sharp tone of a highstrung child: "Saran, I'm choked up with sadness . . . " — "Thanks for lying, my lovely . . . " Soum feels obliged to intervene: "Marie-Astrid has developed the inventory of her connections too well . . . And Saran, unfortunately, has no sense of humor . . . " Stupidity pontificating. Camara bursts out in nervous laughter. The car teeters uncomfortably. I find myself with my head on Aminata's chest, my left hand on her legs. Marie-Astrid screams bloody murder. Still, the car has stabilized nicely. "Brilliant, don't you think?" — "Camara, just drive." — "That's what I'm doing, my dear Soum, and artfully, too . . . " — "You're as fast as a black cabdriver. That's a compliment." — "Soum, you are a bizarre kind of racist for an African. Do you dislike yourself that much?" — "For the revolution you make do with what you have. I've seen quite a bit of the people . . . But the black man . . . takes the cake . . . Ready for colonization again, to be put on the railroad tracks. Look where you're going, brother. I'd like to live through recolonization before I croak." Between her outbursts of hilarity, Marie-Astrid yells out stridently: "You are an exterminating angel, Soum; balls . . . " — "A bit vulgar there, don't you think? What do you say, Camara?" — "The ideas you have, Soum . . . Anything to divert anyone . . . As for vulgarity . . . " — "My ideas? You hear that, Saran? As if I didn't believe in these damned Negroes! I am one, for God's sake! But do we know how to do anything? One, two, at three, laugh! Please . . . Three . . . We know, we know. One: how to steal, from the bottom to the top, including the proletarians . . . at the first opportunity, just grab . . . Two: how to dance . . . cha-cha-cha, rumba . . . What do you think we'll be doing after dinner? Just like everyone else in this fine republic, Saturday night, go dancing . . . olé . . . Three: how to fuck . . . fuck . . . always fucking . . . Like animals in heat. So kids, we have some time to go before we manage to change things around. Or better yet, we should teach this nation of slouchers to unlearn stealing, dancing, and fucking . . . " Silence. Then, suddenly, Camara reacts: "Soum . . . cut the shit!"

I am protected, lying across Aminata's chest. She is a mango tree . . . Solid. And tender. The jolts of the car. My body and hers, dangling, the two parts of a chorus in distress. However uncomfortable she may have been, she put her right arm around my shoulders. It makes me sentimental. Finally, I am getting my share. Naked language. A breath. A tacit agreement in the middle of a lesson in materialism. I notice how happy I am. In ten years, I will say to her: "Amina, do you remember that time, in the car, on the way to the airport . . . "

VI

From the moment I woke up there was sweet joviality in the air. It was eleven a.m. A shiver ran through me, inside of me: "I am the happiest of men . . . " This siren song of happiness made me get even with the infernal circles of the preceding days: since yesterday I have the feeling that I'm a torch in the darkness. And last night my friends really knew it, too; they were all over me with their laughter and with questions. I think I drank a good deal less than I usually do. A subterfuge was needed to help me see the light: a hand around my neck was all it took to instill my flesh with joy. All of a sudden, Marie-Astrid's irritating bird noises had begun to sound like a nightingale's song; the triviality of Camara's remarks became instead the expression of exemplary masculinity; Saran's rude silence was now a sign of discretion and dignity; Soum's exasperating condescension became a form of good-heartedness . . . I was in seventh heaven. Aminata's mood had changed again: she was talking loudly, slapping her thighs: "I tell you, you're a bunch of maniacs . . . " Even though there had to be an age difference of several years, I could feel that she matched me perfectly, both in the rhythm of our breathing and in my newly found high spirits. "Saran, you are a queen . . . give me another hug . . . "—"Nara is actually loosening up, he really is . . . " —"Since you're about to leave us anyway, might just as well let the little flame show . . . " Peels of bell-like laughter . . . Her small, hard eyes were sparkling . . . She was saying her good-byes . . . Immigration, customs. Then she was gone.

The restaurant, a long room with chrome lighting. Rows of tables . . . White tablecloths . . . A rose in the center of each one. A geometrically perfect, artificial garden. The walls covered in red velvet . . . Soum and I are the first customers. Camara drove the women home to change. "A table for five. We'll wait for our friends at the bar." I yield. Above all, I tell myself, hold on to this deep sense of well-being . This evening I am changing my attitude. Soum, paternal, led me to a small private room . . . "Would you like a drink, gentlemen?"—"Yes . . . Nara, what will you have?"—"Whatever you're having . . . "—"Let me suggest a cocktail from the islands. You'll like it. Two planter's, please." It tasted like a star exploding . . . Warm . . . No, tepid rather . . . Slightly tart, despite a sugary aftertaste. I'm beginning to slide deep into the armchair when a bolt of lightning cuts through my chest. Recovered, I allow the planter's enchantment with its discreet aroma of rum to pass through me. Soum is watching me with a glint in his eye. "And?"—"It's great!" I give him thumbs up to prove it.

The others were arriving. An aura of suggestive perfumes. Long multicolored dresses. Perfect for the restaurant's pretentious style. They settled down for their drinks. Soum again suggested planter's . . . Marie-Astrid shrieked at the top of her voice: "At this rate we'll be smashed in an hour, Soum! Is that what you're hoping for?"—"If that's what you want, it's your business . . . " Sarcastically, Camara broke the spell: "A planter's for me . . . To keep Soum company in his mourning . . . To console me for Saran's departure . . . " A whiskey for Marie-Astrid . . . A martini for Aminata . . . Everyone was caught up in the growing buoyancy . . . I remember only the splendor: chandeliers, china, wines, hearty laughter, delicious dishes. And there, in the middle of the circle, the rose, glowing with health. "Wouldn't it be terrific to have a party like this every night

... " — "Marie-Astrid certainly stands up for black tradition, doesn't she? I bet that in the Socialist universe . . . " — "Partying doesn't exist . . . " — "Camara! spoilsport! Doesn't socialism really mean a full bowl for everyone?" — "You'll see, Marie-Astrid, as time goes on . . . " A struggle had become a game . . . Words are undoing the seams of connectedness . . . Though not feigned, indignation causes no concern at all, does not make way for anger . . . "The bottom line is that motherhood is the only thing that counts . . . " — "And wealth?" — "Why do you assume that it is that same inspector again?" — "In any event, at the library we are all for the unlimited right to strike . . . " — "That will depend on the boss . . . " Aminata has found the warmth of her voice again. With each sentence she unveils a flower bed of unknown blooms. There is discretion in what she is saying, moderation, a little bit of fear, at least a delicate restraint . . . Each step may, indeed, expose a thigh . . . "She is the heiress to her maternal grandfather's steel industry . . . That is rare, in keeping with the customs . . . " — "It isn't necessary to go to the doctor with that complaint . . . A suction cup will remove bad blood . . . You'll be better in less than a week . . . " — "Did you see that bit of sacrilege? Yet another invention of our leaders: planting Indian canna, the ritual tree, all along the avenues at Krishville . . . " — I didn't notice time pass . . . Delightful Epiphany night.

In the restaurant with Isabelle, too, it used to be a ritual. The pleasures of an equally adulterated luxury. But tense in mind and feeling. Even as we left the house, there would always be annoying little arguments about a color of make-up, a neckline to be straightened, or a haircut . . . "It's awful . . . " — "That's because you want it that way . . . " — "If you believe that, it's just because you're mean." — "Are we

97

fighting already? How about waiting till dessert?" Good-natured as she was, she would laugh. And so, the trek would be chaotic, perverse. The joy lay in removing the brambles, discovering the innocence either in remorse or violence. Gestures of love thus became exquisite pearls lost in the bumps and the residue of fallow land. On a regular basis, getting through an evening began to feel like having time to kill in the middle of a storm. Passion, an expedient stratagem, was becoming a product of reason by fitting into a complicated staging on every single occasion.

In the restaurant, while we would exchange apologies of sorts, thereby exorcising the dread of our mutual attraction, I would tick off the hour that would follow upon our return to her apartment . . . She puts the key in the lock . . . She is panting, proclaims how tired she feels . . . It is a threat . . . My mother comes running . . . I put my arm around her shoulders, push her gently . . . With the delicate care required for a woman who has just given birth . . . I close the door with my foot . . . I lead her to an easy chair . . . Her pain? The sound of desire . . . But it is up to me to pretend to be obsessed . . . Her denials confirm the opposite is true . . . "A nightcap?" — "No . . . , I really don't want one . . . " — "Even if I have one?" — "Well, then, of course . . . " I'll serve us two large scotches . . . I'll have mine and make sure to make it come alive: I'll seat myself in the circle of light and absentmindedly I'll create the birth of the ice cubes' chant, lost between the whiskey and a thin layer of water . . . I approach, chest straight, and an indecisive look . . . I am an ambivalent shadow . . . And an insolent one . . . I see that she is more flushed than usual . . . The excitement, obviously . . . "Isabelle, let me caress your breasts . . . " — "If you want to . . . "

A facet. A mirror. The beginning of existence at every bend. It was like a card game: to know how to anticipate what is held inside beyond the appearances of things. With Aminata in my arms at the Maxine Club, there was no war I was leaving behind, no games I had to play . . . I was giddy with the music, the softened light, and her perfume, melted into tones of sweat. Never yet had I inhabited such a peaceful space. The dry lines of my heart had become blurred . . . From the details of this illumination arises a memory: I am dancing with Aminata . . . She presses me close. I circle around slowly, my arm around her waist, my eyes lost in the distance . . . "Are you happy, Nara?" — "I adore you, Aminata . . . " — "Don't be foolish . . . You're not falling in love with me, I hope?" — "Are you afraid of that?" — "That's not the problem . . . You need me . . . I accept you like that, Nara . . . But you don't love me . . . You can't . . . " — "Are you forbidden territory, Amina?" — "Come now . . . , you know very well that I'm not, Nara . . . " Mike Brant gives me something to think about . . . I recoil from the promise of that fusion . . .

> *Without a thought, I asked you*
>
> *to come and dance with me*
>
> *to give me time to touch your hands*
>
> *without a thought, I looked for you*
>
> *without a thought, I will be loving you . . .*

Our hearts opened up. The sounds of abundance thrill me . . . We are circling in the sun . . . The infinite number of circles hums, innumerable feelings in incandescent light . . .

I glide through sensual delights, my head high, and gentle-mouthed . . .

> *Let me love you one whole night*
>
> *Let me take you on a longest*
>
> *a loveliest trip for one whole night*
>
> *You know you want that too . . .*

A thin thread of saliva makes me aware of my mouth. I quietly get rid of it. Aminata's neck is lined with wrinkles . . . They're filling up with drops of sweat. Shimmering like precious stones. Between my trembling and her silence everything seemed like a continuous cry to me . . . "Amina, why did you come to me?" — "I'm wondering that myself . . . " I moved away from her a little and looked her in the eyes . . . I caught an astonished candor there. I took her in my arms again, a bit more firmly . . . "But that's absurd, Amina . . . What were you looking for?" — "Maybe to clear my conscience . . . I don't know, Nara . . . " — "Don't you love me?" — "What a question!" She seemed deeply shocked . . . She stiffened briefly . . . A wall . . . "Amina, you picked me up . . . you really did . . . Why?" — "Yes, indeed . . . Why?" I felt the pressure of her arms very clearly, a light kiss on my forehead . . . I was becoming incapable of naming my own temptations. She wasn't laughing at me . . . That was very clear. But she was protecting me from my dreams. Her affection justified her lack of constraint. She gave freely of herself. But I certainly had no right to throw myself on the beach of her expectations . . . "Picked you up, Nara? . . . What a way of putting it! Tell me, does

one pick up one's own son? Please, hold me a little closer
. . ."

Marshland. Once again, I'm adrift in lethargy. The African independencies were rising more firmly on the horizon. There had been France's wager . . . with or without me . . . From one day to the next, I had become, as had most of my African friends, a kind of celebrity. There were endless appeals. I fled from the university. Truly . . . I had no desire to play some sort of revolutionary hero. Cioran had immunized me: "There is no point in either refusing or accepting the social order: we are forced to submit to its changes, for better or for worse, with a desperate conformity, just as we submit to birth, love, climate, and death."

Political vigor, Dr. Sano, is the most gratuitous of passions, the most harmful one, too . . . The Nation to be created, the State to be defended or protected are translucent concepts . . . Africa would have been better off without States . . . I sought refuge in the Pussycat-Bar . . . There I could attempt to grasp the immensity of the symbols . . . For my dreams . . . a piece of the rue Gay-Lussac, the Renovasec dry cleaners, a pharmacy at the corner of the rue Royer-Collard, always lit up . . . A bakery at the entry to the alley . . . I pile on layers and layers, for hours on end, and am astounded that I can still get angry . . . "Tell me, Dr. Sano, what's the use of a revolution in Africa? Soum has a big heart: he works so that we may enter a state of uninterrupted vacation . . . But he feels despair . . . In Africa, hope may not be mentioned . . . It makes its appearance in the spotlight of questionability and duplicity . . . " It is Isabelle, I think, who taught me to flee from these missions pulsating with blood . . . After she . . . picked me up . . . We saw each other again at the Pussycat-Bar. She keeps me from demeaning myself . . . And within a week I pull myself together. Only very rarely now do I give in to the irresistible call that used to condemn me to the boulevard Saint-Michel in the evenings. I would go back and forth until I was ready to drop, searching and waiting for a human voice . . . For years I lived like that . . . "Almost every evening, Dr. Sano, up and down the boulevard, from the place Saint-André to the gare du Luxembourg and from there back to the place. When I'd run into a friend, I would patiently explain that I was walking my dinner off. Obviously, nobody believed me. I was stuck in mire. Inexorably . . . I couldn't even put an end to it anymore. Are you familiar with the taste of death, Dr. Sano? For your sake, I hope not. Pounding the pavement night after night, a bitter taste in your mouth, your stomach in knots and burning. Waiting for the fleeting pleasure of some passerby who might acknowledge your existence . . . making do with that, knowing that thereby another month has been added to your life . . . Death, Dr. Sano, I tell you. You watch yourself being split, devoted to illusions, a false hopelessness, the pretext . . . the refusal to live. It is true, I have narrow hips and a solid behind. With time I learned to use them, reasons for challenge. But never, Dr. Sano, was I able to overcome them . . . " One Christmas night, as I'm going up Saint-Michel, there's a scuffle at the crosswalk of Saint-Germain, a push . . . and I fall. Someone bends over me and I hear a woman's voice: "Pardon me, sir, are you hurt?" — "No, I don't think so. It's nothing, thank you . . . " She offers me her hand, helps me get up: "Come with me." And, Dr. Sano, I followed her . . . just like that . . . I was an obedient little dog. She took me to the Cluny and sat down across from me. "Have something hot. A toddy." "No thank you, but thank you all the same." — "A scotch? A beer?" — "A beer would be nice. You are very kind."

What strikes me are her eyes. A temperate climate.

Calm waters. The smell of the sea. And then, too, her uncontrollable hair; her full mouth . . .

"My name is Isabelle Colmeur." — "Ahmed Nara." — "Are you a student?" — "Yes, in history." — "I'm in contemporary literature. Today is Christmas . . . " — "I've noticed. Is that important to you?" — "I'm Catholic." — "I see. I'm Muslim. Well, not totally. I don't believe in it . . . I think because of my education; I studied in a Catholic high school." — "Let's celebrate Christmas together, Ahmed . . . Do you want to?"

The anchor . . . She had a key in her hand . . . A door swung open, another one . . . A Christmas tree . . . Chocolate pieces . . . An enormous turkey . . . Jars with nougat . . . A bottle of champagne . . .

And this morning it was Aminata, who, in the name of her affection for me, forced me to attend a Protestant service. "Shall we go, Nara?" — "Why? After all, I'm a Muslim . . . " — "Come and watch . . . It'll keep you occupied. And it will make me happy to be with you."

Like a good lapdog I went along, giving up the possibility of a lazy morning at home in exchange for the shouting of an impassioned preacher.

I attended the service by completely ignoring it. I had entered a no-man's-land, my body hidden, my thoughts turned in upon themselves. A dance of gestures and chants . . . I was contemplating all those necks . . . Almost all of them looked vulnerable . . . Rising out of faded suits, out of dresses with starched collars. Many heads of white hair. Long skirts, interminably long. " . . . Ananias, why has Satan conquered your heart to the extent that you lie to the Holy Spirit and keep back so much on the price of your field . . . "

A mirage begins. The bricks red as fire have the evil eye . . . Shining . . . Without number . . . Straight rows . . .

Lines that move farther and farther apart from each other
. . . Inert and babbling . . . Then a whole wall of them . . .
A human tide . . . Closed faces . . . Piety . . . "They call us
God's children and so we are." All looks converge upon the
pathetic clown. Gesticulating. Should I get out of here?
This violence of speech leaves words riveted to metaphors.
The white wings of a surplice swim above the crowd. The
smell of people in the air. A chair creaks behind me. A
woman's small cough responds. I say to myself: is this conspicuous silence as important as the symbols that call it
forth? Aminata is a prisoner. Just as the others are. Con-
gealed. Dismayed. Hard. Her jaws clenched. Below the
northern triforium, the white billows of the choir robes.
"Lord, show us the Father, that will suffice unto us . . . "
Well . . . on the path of my insolence the call wasn't even
objectionable any longer. To my left, Aminata welcomed it
with composure. And yet, she knew as well as I did how all
of this was pure entertainment for Soum . . . Religion, the
opium . . . Metaphors were decomposing in this framework. It was too faithful a reflection. Give me your spirit
so I may defile it. There will be no more door frames. The
shutters have been taken down. Fruit ripens without pits.
And the crowd hovers at the edge of life. No movement. A
silent, compact tide all along the nave, wallowing in a few
unbelievable, obvious statements . . . "I have not come on
my own, it is the Father who has sent me . . . I shall not say
to you that I will pray to the Father for you, for the Father
Himself loves you . . . The Spirit comes to help us in our
weakness . . . for we know not what to ask in our prayers
. . . But the Spirit itself intercedes for us through its unut-
terable moans . . . "

The preacher was clapping his hands. The congrega-
tion became inflamed, inspired, melting with enthusiasm. I
was moved and felt a stranger to this proclamation of

Christ. "The greatest catastrophe for this nation, Nara, is Jesus Christ. In him the whole structure of African irrationality has been reconciled . . . " Soum, as usual, seemed like a schoolmaster . . . "The patina of Negro traditions on the Messiah from Israel . . . The finest jewel of colonialization . . . A masterful crossbreeding . . . Heads bowed down under its weight . . . Total victory . . . We do know something about that in the Party . . . Dialectical materialism is slowly disintegrating . . . slowly . . . And yet, it is the only thing that can set us free . . . "

Bitterness. He thought that he could open a window onto hope, came up against a surprise. What hope? "I really do understand, Soum, in your own way you're playing the prophet."—"Are you sure you're all right, Nara?"— "Yes, indeed, Soum. Very well, in fact. Hope, all hope, is characteristic of slaves . . . " Hallelujas burst forth. Aminata is singing, her voice is frail, coming from deep in her throat. In this flood time stands still. Characteristic of slaves? She had her heaven to testify to my misery. I am convinced that she was aware of my reluctance. With the eyes of a sick bird, I put on a sly face. Because of her? She has dimples when she sings . . . And I, I am a patient dog . . . Motionless . . . The memory of the planter's persistent on my tongue . . . "Hold me closer . . . "—"That will keep you occupied . . . "

After the service, we stopped by my former apartment. "Move out . . . It's so much simpler, Nara . . . You can live with me . . . There's certainly enough space."

The landlord wasn't even surprised. I was expecting an outcry, protestations. "Of course, Mr. Nara. You have already paid for the month. Still, it's a pity . . . You know, the air-conditioning is working perfectly now. But tell me one thing, were you raising rats . . . or what?"

Images. Hallways again. Fortunately, well lighted. Here and there some masks. Aminata disappears. She's packing my bags. Embarrassment. Moist lips, I must put one foot in front of the other . . . Floor tiles in sandstone . . . A dead rat . . . I jump over him . . . On the left, a stuffed owl instead of a mask. It upsets the order. I am undoubtedly in the wrong not to understand the arrangement of the scraped and polished setting. Without my having sought her out, a blonde nurse comes forward. "Watch out, Isabelle . . . A rat."—"Where?"—"There, behind your bookcase."—"We'll take care of him this evening. Put your suitcase over there. It's heavy. Let's get the boxes from the cab."—"I still don't see the point of intruding into your life like this."—"It's more practical, Nara. It saves time and money."

You offer me a permanent pasture. Demons are living inside us and we are learning to enjoy them. The taboos are disappearing. We fasten our relationship to a foundation of obsession. I immediately ask you out to the Cluny to commemorate our first encounter. Your white T-shirt annoys me . . . I don't yet dare to push you around . . . It fits you tightly, molding to your chest . . . Below your breasts everyone can read: "I'm frustrated, Inhibited, And no one understands me." With your black servant? Or because of him? My breath begins to come more haltingly . . .

Aminata has packed everything. A groove is emptied. This time, too, I am worried about leaving. A taxi. An old fear is rising. I try to hide it. This departure is a repetition of an earlier one . . . I was stretched out across a street in the middle of the night . . . There were legs here and there on my broken body . . . They're scraping the ground . . . Tiny women's shoes . . . Very light . . . Stiletto heels . . . White . . . Orange . . . Green . . . Black . . . Two-toned . . . Hard shoes with laces, with elastic, with buttons . . . The footsteps of a man, heavy, slow . . . The boot . . . Heavy soles . . . The step of a hobnailed boot . . . The tap of the dancing-shoe . . . Dance of colors . . . There is the enemy, his feet shod. If I don't get up quickly . . . A voice comes to my aid: "Please get up, please . . . Excuse me . . . Come with me . . . " A hand. Cracking of bones. The bumping of the car beat time to the horror of my escape. "Dr. Sano, one needs a considerable dosage of thoughtlessness to devote oneself to no matter what, without any further consideration." — "Is this your own idea?" — "Almost. It's embedded in my skin. But the expression is Cioran's." — "Against Isabelle?" — "Against her or anyone, against faith and love, against politics and science. They're innocent games of emptiness and loss, Dr. Sano." — "And death, Nara, death as well?" — "Death is not a truth, Dr. Sano." — "Really?" — "In every conviction I have seen a defilement and in every attachment a desecration." — "Are you quoting Cioran again?" — "Yes. But he has become inscribed in me. And so I can give new passion to my own despair. The supreme nostalgia is my death." — "You devise it by proxy . . . What if you were to reverse the perspective, Nara . . . is life a truth? You cannot lose. Give it a try . . . "

I certainly was losing. Aminata's brazen body. Her effusive wish to pave a road for me. She wasn't even stirring my curiosity. She is too much a follower of the cult of life. She suggests its meanings. And so I am dazzled by the anecdote she calls forth. Yes, that's it, Aminata is an inn. My suitcases are here now. To unpack them would be a sign. I prefer to wait for a dream.

She is full of attentions that imply something, more and more awkward in her displays. "Take a tranquilizer, Nara. You are so tense." — "What are you afraid of?" — "You aren't well . . . " My anguish lays claim to my body . . . I am beyond reach . . . I give up.

A Sunday afternoon in Krishville . . . Outside, bar music . . . Strollers in luxurious boubous . . . And there I am, cornered between a woman, a door, and a window. In pieces. The sky hangs low. The rain could come tonight. "So, the body of death, what is it?"—"Arms, legs, a nude torso . . . nothing else, Dr. Sano."—"I don't understand."—"An extraordinary body, Dr. Sano. It saves you from everything. From the night, the rats, women."— "Even from Isabelle, Nara? Careful, Nara . . . remember. The beginning . . . Her tongue . . . Her eyes . . . You loved her eyes . . . The eyes of life itself . . . Tell me about her eyes."—"Did I talk about them that much? That was pure affectation, Dr. Sano. Her tongue . . . , yes, I remember. Soft, moist, pliant, and cold . . . A snake . . . very small . . . very pointy. I have to close my eyes because I'm afraid of it . . . I'm going to scream . . . I stop kissing her . . . I'm in a cold sweat . . . It is a winter evening . . . The day after Christmas . . . The heat is barely working. The veins on her arms are blue. She gets undressed, throws her blouse carelessly on a low stool, unbuttons her slacks . . . I'm looking at the window. When I turn around, she is naked. She is smiling at me, comes toward me, and begins to undo my clothes. I am petrified . . . And then her mouth opens . . . " —"But her body, Nara . . . It is there against yours . . . You feel it . . . you react . . . Remember . . . "—"I remember it well, Dr. Sano, very well indeed . . . Her body smells of death . . . Yes . . . exactly . . . The smell of curdled milk left out in the sun . . . "—"Yet, you did continue to live with her . . . "—"Yes, that is the miracle . . . the union of hatred, death, and love . . . Love . . . Dr. Sano . . . "

Aminata is keeping busy in the kitchen. I have been to the bathroom to comb my hair. The mirror reflected my face. Red eyes, unkempt hair . . . The image of my thinking? A door slams . . . The wind . . . and the dusk . . . The day is ending. Death takes over. And I recall the words of one of Suzanne Allen's heroines: "To take strict care that death be punctual is possible only through the formula 'to expose the light of day' of the great sibylline incest. A contorted death, a death as tight as a young girl's genitals, a maiden death, one that never again will take place. Innocence that obstructs the way, that must be perforated to free the blood, the meaning."

The night has come . . . It completes its hollowness. I'm looking for a nest . . . Like the pastor this morning with his tales of the Father . . . Cornered . . . And above all, there is still the long evening that lies before me. Dear God, what to do!

VII

Feel as if I'm in mourning. Tracks, on a deserted beach . . . I follow them. The sand. The monstrous sea. Distant waves, very blue, edged in white. I'm calling. Loudly. The echo of my voice. I'm screaming. It's no use. Sometimes there are minuscule drops of blood in the hollows left by footprints. What brings me to this desert is the note written down in my notebook that I found again. Nietzsche? Sartre? Cioran? " . . . even the proudest heartbeats are swallowed up by the sewer where they stop beating, as if they had reached their natural limit: this downfall constitutes the drama of the human heart and the negative meaning of history . . . "

A river. Opaque. Stinking . . . At least the day will have brought some progress. From eight in the morning until six in the evening I worked without interruption, prey to a veritable rage: to reconstruct the course of the Kuba as best and as quickly as possible. Is it an attempt to create a world? Or, more simply, am I possessed? I skipped lunch because of it, declining Aminata's invitation. The hypocrite. Always around me . . . As if that would have any meaning! She wanted me in a cage. I am there. Now I'll bring her to the point where she'll name her own lies. All of them, without exception . . . That ascetic Protestant who opened her charitable arms to a lost soul. "Dr. Sano, explain something to me, you who are a believer . . . Charity . . . All throughout secondary school I heard them talk about it. Isabelle, is that charity?" — "I don't know, Nara. The problem lies elsewhere. Are you a child?" — "Not anymore. I was the best of kids. With a mother like mine . . . And then, too: try to act like a child with Catholic missionaries . . . Especially since they were dreaming of converting me to their God. No, Dr. Sano, I have never been a child. And then . . . This is important. Can a Negro be a child?"—"You're joking?"—"Are we really just big children, as the Toubab say we are?"—"What do you think, Nara?"

All night long it rained. The air was clear. I had left Aminata right after dinner. Terrible. Turtle in tomato sauce with potatoes. Still, I had eaten very conscientiously. With a full and heavy stomach, I fled into sleep as if I were escaping from something. A trick. Her face looks perplexed . . . A question mark. "Yes, my dear, I'm tired of working . . . I'm going to sleep."—"What's the matter?"—"I'm just sleepy. Is that so strange?"—"Are you trying to get away from me already?"—"God, what a stupid idea! I live here, don't I? . . . " When I left her, her eyes were wet . . .

I picked up my project again. The Kuba forest. I'm itching to move on. The index cards are beginning to fall into place. Bits of old information are starting to make sense. My grassy, marshlike, majestically complex fresco is beginning to take shape . . . I'm going to be able to start writing the text. In five days? Perhaps even sooner. First I have to put all the data in order. Several times I felt Aminata's eyes on me. Four or five times she went to the window . . . Could she not be feeling well?

I am in the center of a geyser . . . The splendor of the spring. My thoughts are ahead of me. My body has disappeared. From time to time, I feel my tongue caressing my teeth . . . They must be mine . . . I have renounced my own greed. I enter into the history of the Kuba . . . My project has become as broad as day. I am climbing the sun's rays. A thick, warm, malleable matter ... Grafting wax that smells of honey and turpentine ... The walls turn around ... The limpid sea ... Between the blue of the sky and the tenderness of the sand there are my footsteps populating the silence ... A few notes of music ... The cry of a wood owl. The scratching of my pen on paper. "Dr. Sano, I live in constant terror."—"Do you encounter something specific? No matter what. A voice, a gesture, a hammer, sirens?"—"Only the sun ... And still" ...—"What does that mean?"—"Like rays. Illuminations. They burn ... I wonder why I'm not on fire."—"You're not made of fire?"—"No. I don't think so. I would like to have been fire. Do you understand that, Dr. Sano? The intensity of the truth that destroys ... "—"Does truth destroy?"—"It absorbs, Dr. Sano, it consumes, it uses you up until you are wiped out. The truth is exhausting, Dr. Sano."

That was during my last conversation with him. Nine days ago. My appointment with him for tomorrow afternoon doesn't promise much anymore. It's more like boredom. My morning's work had chained me to what is of the essence: the Kuba destiny ... Indestructible ... "In politics, the truth is the opposite of lying ... Try and figure out one side as opposed to the other ... Especially in politics ... One of my Communist friends, Soum, you know of him ... makes it into an improved condition ... Pretty, right? Tempting, isn't it? But wrong, all wrong, Dr. Sano. Truth is fire and all around it is emptiness."—"Nietzsche or Cioran?"—"Neither. That's me. Nietzsche was content with mortal truths and was astonished that nobody dies of those any longer. That's just like him. It makes you understand how he ended."—"That is to say?"—"Smoke ... Black smoke ... The opposite of the sun's rays ... Do you understand?"—"Yes?"—"Look ... history as spirit, despite its precariousness and fragility . . . is a bit like that . . . the mystery of the match . . . " — "You're piling up your difficulties, Nara." — "You think so? It's more like clarifying the issues. And then there is the Kuba miracle. It will save me from Isabelle, from all the lies. Then I can burn up . . ."

The promise was no longer an allusion. Isabelle, Aminata's place; the other side, the black side of the symbol. The sash had unrolled very rapidly. Once the forces were joined, I had promised myself to name the new line of understanding. In the taxi that took us home at the end of the day, Aminata looked tired. I was stripped. More precisely, I felt emptied out and perceived myself as stripped to the bone. The fabulous succession of Kuba annals had burst forth into a spectacle that sent me reeling back to my misery. "What's the big news, Aminata?" — "The strike . . . The bank employees have gotten started. In the administrative services they're still wavering. The usual pressure. And especially the blackmail." — "Didn't you see Soum at noon? I'd like to hear his opinion." — "He phoned early in the afternoon to ask after you." — "And what about the strike?" — "He says it's shit. That is a direct quote. You understand . . . An increase in salaries . . . He thinks that's inane. He would like to see a general strike where the first demand is one that establishes the rights of workers and peasants." — "I don't mean to pry, but you said 'to ask after me' . . . what's that supposed to mean?" — "How you are, what you're up to . . . "

She was watching me, staring in the dark. Her eyes shining, too. The car went in the direction of the airport. After three miles we would get back on the road to Krishville. I was intrigued by Soum's concern for me. Such discretion! And yet . . . A threshold to be crossed . . . I watched her, with expectation, showing no emotion, but really I was in desperate straits. She was lying. That was clear. Obvious. I felt a rising terror. I reacted quickly, crushed it as effectively as a quick scare chases the hiccups. Aminata began to press against me. She was stretching her arm out to touch me. I drew back, pretending not to notice. Her approach and my recoil were shaken with each jolt of the ride. Suddenly I felt her knee against my thigh . . . "Give me your hand, Nara . . . " — "Here, mother . . . "

And I held it out to her, palm up, fingers widely spread.

An airport tower on the horizon . . . Did I really see it? I crouched back. Krishville came to meet us. We were sucked up. Its face is closed. Did it have to break up into black prisms? A road with potholes. Streetlights bent in the earlier riots. So they say . . . The ground is soaking wet. My head against the car door. The springs are creaking. And I, cutting deals with the future . . . Brilliant . . .

I woke up around ten in the evening. Aminata and the children were sleeping. Complete quiet. Unable to get back to sleep, I decided to write. Here is my future, in this solitary night. The house across the street is dark. A very small yellow light at the front door. A pack of dogs is barking somewhere. I am walking through the interminable night . . . A tunnel . . . Facades of buildings, plastered with oil and filth . . . I come from no place . . . Surely, there have been secret seasons interspersed with rainy seasons . . . Undefined roads wrecked by successive winters, and I am walking between heaven and earth . . . I avoid the tracks, as I do this evening . . . At last, I'm going to confront myself, penetrate the night . . . To be a night-destroyer at last, the craftsman of my adventure as well as of the illusions I will run across.

I am choosing myself . . . and I opt for this night, this rat's nest.

"Shall we dance? Aren't you tired yet . . . " It's a beach . . . The surface of the sea gets darker. "Isabelle, look, sea gulls. White spots on deep blue. There, on your left . . . " Strangled doe . . . "Is this a joke, Aminata? Holding me tight like this?" — "So what? You heard Soum . . . I love to dance." — "Yes, we Negroes . . . " — "No, you and I. Your theories . . . make me tired." — "Like a magical object . . . " Your black eyes . . . Her blue eyes on the red background of a pauper's grave . . . I'm talking gibberish, that's for sure. But since when? There is my anger or my viciousness . . . toward Aminata. Unless it's toward Isabelle. Insignificant, obviously. That is what's abnormal: my inability to really embrace them.

I went as far as the window. An occasional star. In the distance . . . Ocher . . . Innocent? This night I understand that even hope grows old. It cannot survive me. How do I tell this to Soum? When I wanted to clarify my doubts about the universality of his method to him, he quoted Marx to me: The relationships of production form a whole, which in no way implies that history is a totality, but it does imply that there are totalities within history. A talisman for Africa? And resentment fits that mold very well. Tears also. Isabelle's and Aminata's tears. Neither motivated nor dialectical . . . My shivering too, as night approaches. "Dr. Sano, anguish blows . . . Yes, just like the wind. The night's embrace brings it to life . . ." — "You should really overcome that . . . " — "Overcome the night . . . How? Tell me how and I promise you that I'll follow your advice word for word. I am surrounded by the night. Life is there, but it is dead . . . silent. Trees, flowers, insects . . . All that is breathing. All that is alive. And I am completely drowned in it. I'm going to step on a scorpion. Or on a dead rat. Or I'm going head first into a tree and rip open my forehead. Tell me, Dr. Sano, what is it that I should overcome . . . "

In the precise measure of her violence, Isabelle had a much lighter touch. In that first encounter at the Cluny, she was really taking revenge for her lonely Christmas night . . . My falling down had allowed her to create a new night for herself . . . Like Aminata the night before last . . .

"How's your beer?" — "It's good, thanks." — "You like beer?" — "Yes, well, it's a habit. Because of the heat. It does refresh you. That can't be denied . . . And then, too . . . it doesn't go to your head. That is, you'd need an awful lot of it . . . " — "Tell me about yourself." — "Oh, my God! . . . What am I supposed to say . . . "

A blow . . . a feeling . . . A past . . . hideous . . . The turmoil of a miserable childhood . . . A brainwashing they call education . . . Some vague studying of history . . . A diploma . . . The anus open to the explosion of haphazard lovers . . . And then getting to like men . . . "My life is nothing special. Really. You don't believe me? An ordinary youth, some university training. Yes . . . history. No involvements with women." — "That's impossible . . . " — "No, it isn't, Isabelle." — "Another beer?" — "No, not yet. You want to dance, don't you? Aminata, hold me tight . . . Otherwise I'll threaten . . . to fall in love with you . . . " — "What a joke! Come, you big bum . . . " — "Like that, Aminata . . . You do love playing mother? I am your doll . . . Is that it? No? Well, I really thought so . . . I'm not lying to you. I've had a perfectly ordinary childhood, a perfectly ordinary adolescence . . . " — "Really, no affairs?" — "I swear. Well, of course there's Isabelle." — "Isabelle?" — "Yes. Isabelle. That's you, you know . . . Oh . . . yes . . . " — "Are you going to tell me about her?" — "But I know you so little, Aminata, how can I tell you about yourself?"

The music is restrained. Camara is dancing with Marie-Astrid. Soum, solitary and ambiguous, is yawning. Marie-Astrid told him that he was a misfit in the group because he had no woman . . . As she said it, she was looking at me, a malicious glint in her eye. If she only knew . . . "Can you read what it says on my forehead?" — "No, obviously not." — "Try." — "I can't." — "Yes you can."

You're laughing and I notice your teeth, solidly set. Though lightly yellowed, they still have the force of hard ivory. I try to guess your age. Ecstasy imbues me. "I see in your face that we're going to get along beautifully." — "You think so? But I've told you that I've never been with a woman before. I'm a virgin, if you must know. Strange for a man my age, isn't it?" — "It's Christmas . . . Nara, you'll be my Emmanuel . . . " — "But you didn't beget me . . . " — "No, that is true . . . But I did pick you up . . . "

Isabelle, Aminata . . . The night suffers because of them. The gulf . . . The abyss . . . Mosquitoes . . . Sewage smells . . . The parade of creatures in a mob . . . And I stay up for a funeral march whose sign I vainly seek. It was my mother. A very long time ago, something to do with a whim, long lost in the past. "You can't always have it your way in life, Nara . . . " I never forgot that . . . That's why I'm here, busy reconstructing my life. I just went to the refrigerator. I drank a large glass of water. I brought some back to my room. On the kitchen table lay a teaspoon. I took it. Automatically. The glass (?) sits here in front of me. I am practicing patience and self-discipline. Five written lines will give me the right to have a spoonful of water . . .

" . . . Dr. Sano . . . I wonder . . . It's the daytime that is abnormal. It's a deletion. The text of life is black. No matter what written text proves that. Erase the black. And you will understand that letters kill. The night is a letter. Like the Negro. Tell me which fault of his it is that can explain his degradation." — "Take a piece of white chalk. There is one on my desk, over there. Take it and write something on the blackboard." — "No thanks. Just a game of tic-tac-toe. That's like politics. Are you political, Dr. Sano? I hate politicians." — "I suppose you do." — "Because I can also write with my blood. One little cut, a pen, and a white sheet of paper is all it takes . . . That's it, red ink . . . That's all it takes, Dr. Sano . . . "

Was he displeased with me? That last session had been unusual. Instead of sitting at his desk, he had been in back of me, sunken away in a couch. A pasha . . . He was wearing a new suit . . . Sky blue . . . He hadn't changed his jacket for a white coat as he usually did . . . Another twist: he had lit a cigarette and was leafing through a women's fashion magazine. I could imagine part of his dreams . . . as he looked at some spellbinding and glorious gown. Isabelle coiled up inside of it, her hair loose and undone . . . And there I was like an idiot, neck tense, sitting on a chair facing an empty desk . . . Nothing on it . . . Made of plain wood . . . A soiled desk pad falling apart . . . The only view: an overgrown garden . . . "You are afraid of me, Dr. Sano . . . That's it, isn't it?" — "I don't think so . . . " — "Then why are you sitting behind me? You could put a knife in my back . . . Isabelle would have . . . I'm sure of it . . . And so are you . . . "

A winding road . . . "Crickets," she says. In the distance the lights of a village in Haute-Vienne. Her short breathing warm on my neck. I turn around suddenly. Her eyes are glowing embers. "Isabelle!" — "Nara . . . I'm furious . . . That stupid breakdown . . . " — "I had nothing to do with it, you can see that, can't you?"—"Oh that! What's the matter with you? Tired? Anyway, we're there . . . There are the lights . . . We'll deal with the car tomorrow." Of course. But the memory of those transfigured eyes . . . And the conviction that a knife in her hands . . . "Have no fear, Nara . . . "—"Thank you . . . Thank you very much . . . So, tell me why you're hiding, Dr. Sano . . . There behind me . . . You are afraid . . . You want to defend yourself . . . That's it, isn't it?"—"Why?"—"Because you think I'm crazy . . . Yes, that's what you think, just like all the rest of them . . . Hypocrites . . . Nara, this . . . Nara, that . . . Behind my back . . . Oh yeah, right . . . Don't deny it, Dr. Sano . . . I wouldn't believe it anyway . . . Besides, I have no confidence in you at all . . . You're lying, Dr. Sano . . . You are always lying to me . . . Always . . . And your statements never mean anything . . ."—"You're not crazy Nara, you're tired . . . "—"Now there's a piece of news . . . I'm tired . . . Big deal . . . Thanks . . . Take a good look at that piece of garden . . . There, in front of me . . . Yes, right there . . . Through the glass door . . . Do you know it at all, Dr. Sano . . . No you don't, right? Because your desk condemns you to turn your back on it . . . You run away from it, every day . . . Run away . . . Neglect it . . . Yes . . . every day . . . That garden is tired, Dr. Sano . . . Those sickly bushes . . . That overgrown piece of grass . . . Turned yellow . . . It's dying of fatigue . . . How long since it was fertilized? . . . A real slum yard . . . You let the weeds grow . . . They've killed the lawn, they were flourishing . . . Then the dry season got to them . . . Now it's their turn . . . They're dying . . . That's your garden, my big man . . . You too, Sano, you make me tired . . . I don't want to die . . . Do you understand, Sano . . . I'm not a blade of grass. And all I have to say to you is: shit . . . "

Above all, don't upset anything in this established order. But where do I take refuge? It's three o'clock in the morning . . . I tear myself away from the window . . . Aminata's eyes, in which my desire becomes iridescent? I try to gauge the shamefulness of my hope . . . Something creaks in the room next to mine . . . Lou and Baka's room . . . They were adorable . . . When Aminata and I came home, they said: "Hi, daddy." It was uncomfortable . . . I made a furtive movement of dismissal . . . Embarrassment? They disappeared . . . This is of a different nature . . . I am their mother's man . . . My detachment is unforgivable . . . I hardly know them . . . What makes them laugh? That's what I miss . . . Curiosity, eagerness . . . Forcing doors open . . . Reassuring them . . . "I'm here, I love you . . . What can I do for you?" Or perhaps seducing them with some excuse . . . "It looks as if you've been having trouble . . . " Then there is the art of playing games . . . "Do I scare you? Look . . . Raise one finger . . . I'll move my head . . . You move your foot . . . I cough . . . Shall we start?"

I long for a future. An abundant future . . . Frenetic. Aminata, to get you out of my system . . . Among the Kuba, the husband offers his dying wife a token: "Here, take this offering . . . go in peace and may your people not persecute me after your death . . . " You belong to the first line of a paragraph . . . You triumph and go under . . . And I am hidden by your sleep . . . Tomorrow, can I still offer you the letter of my body? I will definitely try to separate the heat of the day . . . And then? Isabelle is your skin . . . What worries me is that I'm not sure of it . . . The smell should settle it . . . The day before yesterday, you overwhelmed me with a cologne . . . I imagine you as taut as a bow, your chest thrown out, a female filing away a list of all that I've done . . . I allow myself to take your hand . . . Make a wish

. . . Night is falling . . . The Kuba perimeter is drawn . . . The village prophet has called out your name. It is only proper that I take you to the Tree of the Ancestors. They're calling you there . . . My sister takes us . . . She is wearing a headband; in her hands she is carrying a basket from which three cockscombs emerge . . . She goes forward toward the century-old tree, her step as light as air. A streamer, heavy with an unknown corpse inside, unwinds . . . You scream . . . I am astounded: your attitude creates terror . . . Isabelle is praying to the Ancestors for you, following an old Kuba incantation . . . "Ancient Ones, Mother of our fathers, Father of our grandmothers, accept this, our dwelling . . . May suffering and malediction take their distance from us! May evil remove itself and return to its origin . . . We implore you . . . Grant us the power to continue your lineage . . . " Three days of prayer, with Isabelle as mediator, her heart aflame; three nights on the sleeping mat according to the ancient custom . . . On the last day, the headband(?) was transformed into a lovely strip of porcelain clay all around her head . . . And, sitting beneath the edge of the Tree, you are eating chicken.

It seems to me that I'm climbing those stairs as I'm coming out of this night. Go back . . . Despite everything, I am still fascinated by you . . . Crouched down, your features tense, your face distorted, you heave the evening meal into a yellow basin . . . Your beautiful black skin has white splotches of vomit . . . Slowly you rise, you are looking at me . . . Your inflamed eyes have turned red . . . Poor thing . . . I go to meet you, calmly, planning to kiss your mouth . . . So that you will understand at last . . . And then . . . the expression on your face has changed . . . Just like last night at dinner . . . Those eyes, Aminata . . . Is it just sadness? I have a piece of turtle in my mouth . . . I stop chewing . . . "Yes, they'll repair the car tomorrow . . .

Come, let's head up to the village . . . Give me your hand
. . . " — "Why?" — "Just because, Isabelle . . . I like to hold
hands with you . . . "

Who deserves to be looked at? Give me your hand . . .
Now . . . Right away . . . Again . . . I'm going to match
your breathing . . . Perhaps through your hand I'll feel
what I have always suspected, while I knew it all along . . .
She doesn't open her mouth. The lights are coming closer.
The hotel is on the other side of the station . . . You're lean-
ing into me . . . I'm racking my brain to give a name to that
gesture. You are getting undressed, with a weary look . . . I
am watching the low ceiling . . . A river in the hills is full of
murky water. Your face is wrinkled . . . Your grim look re-
laxes me . . . I notice a cigarette butt in the corner of our
room . . . "Isabelle, stop going around in circles . . . You're
going to get dizzy . . . " — "Thanks, but I already am . . .
For months now . . . In fact, Nara, how many months?" —
"Excuse me?" — "For how many months have you been
making me dizzy now?" — "Oh, my God!"

Naively, I begin to count . . . What is the difference? . . . Being stuck is only an illusion. Just erase me. I discover you to
be caustic. " . . . Nara, we are all death's conscripts . . . " —
"Where did you read that, Aminata?" You burst out laughing, your teeth visible and shining . . . "It was the preacher
. . . It was he who said it, last Sunday, during the service
. . . " — "Do you believe it?" — "Well . . . You know, we are
dancing right now . . . Smile at me, would you . . . " —
"Your preacher, Aminata . . . " — "Yes?" — "He is, as Soum
would say, an antirevolutionary." You laughed and nibbled
at my shoulder. Lightly. Taking possession? It didn't hurt
. . . I kissed your hair . . . It smelled of touchwood. "Aminata, do you know that you look like my mother? No?

Well, it's the honest truth, nevertheless . . . " And I smiled at the insult I thrust upon her.

A light has just been turned on in the street. There, a fingerprint on the turned-over page. My thumb is sweating . . . I listen to my heart . . . No exact statement . . . Yes, perhaps I really am very tired . . . It's almost four in the morning . . . Tomorrow . . . The only thing I have to do: my appointment with Sano . . . My pen begins to skip . . . Let him go to hell . . . His fees for psychotherapy, a shield for a phallic cult . . . And with that he thinks he's working toward the development of this rotten land. I'm going to try to get some rest . . . To be at the library by late morning, rested . . . Have lunch . . . preferably alone . . . Then at least five hours of good hard work . . . Join Soum and Camara in the evening . . . To laugh . . . Yes, that's what I missed tonight . . . To be able to laugh at my delirious outpourings, at last . . . This sense of mourning on a deserted beach . . . And the blood . . . To rediscover how to laugh and to breathe the sea air . . . If only Isabelle and Aminata . . .

V. Y. Mudimbe is currently professor of comparative literature and Romance languages at Duke University. One of Africa's leading intellectuals, he is already an established literary figure in Europe and Africa. He is the author of numerous works of fiction and nonfiction, most of which have been translated into various languages, and is himself the subject of many book-length studies. His *Before the Birth of the Moon* (1989) received many positive reviews in the U.S. media, and *Between Tides*, published in October 1991, won the Grand Prize in France in 1977.

Marjolijn de Jager has translated many works of fiction, among others, V. Y. Mudimbe's *Before the Birth of the Moon* (1989); Ken Bugul's *Abandoned Baobab* (1991); and Assia Djebar's *Women of Algiers in Their Apartment* (1992).